Is Nathan Barrister *your* Millionaire of the Month?

1. It's your job to keep a millionaire content for his month-long stay in town. You

   (a) Fill his house with fresh flowers
   (b) Fill his refrigerator with gourmet goodies
   (c) Fill his mind with thoughts of…you!

2. How to argue with a millionaire:

   (a) You don't
   (b) Gently suggest he might consider someone else's opinion
   (c) Tell him exactly what's on your mind: money doesn't mean a person's always right!

3. You've found yourself stranded with your millionaire in a snowstorm. You

   (a) Throw a log on the fire
   (b) Bundle up in a woolly sweater
   (c) Have two words: bod…

4. Your million… … …of a lifetime. You…

   (a) Accept gle…
   (b) Wait ten sec… …nsider his offer…and th… …eefully
   (c) Turn him dow… You're holding out for a honeymoon!

Dear Reader,

It was very exciting to write the first book in this new series. MILLIONAIRE OF THE MONTH is a continuity that my friends and I came up with, and we had such a great time planning it all out and creating these stories.

The series is set near Lake Tahoe and takes place in and around a mansion built on the shores of the lake. Six men, all once friends in college, are forced to deal with the memories of who they once were when the terms of a seventh friend's will dictate that one of them a month must stay in this lodge to honor a long-ago promise.

My hero, Nathan Barrister, is a man who makes his own rules. He believes in living his life on his terms and never looks back. Keira Sanders, though, is a woman who won't be ignored. She slips into Nathan's life and has no intention of slipping back out again.

I really hope you enjoy the books in this series as much as we did writing them!

Love,

Maureen

THIRTY DAY AFFAIR

MAUREEN CHILD

Silhouette Desire

Published by Silhouette Books
America's Publisher of Contemporary Romance

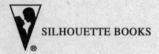

SILHOUETTE BOOKS
®

ISBN-13: 978-0-373-76785-4
ISBN-10:   0-373-76785-4

THIRTY DAY AFFAIR

Recent Books by Maureen Child

Silhouette Desire

Society-Page Seduction #1639
*The Tempting Mrs. Reilly #1652
*Whatever Reilly Wants #1658
*The Last Reilly Standing #1664
**Expecting Lonergan's Baby #1719
**Strictly Lonergan's Business #1724
**Satisfying Lonergan's Honor #1730
The Part-Time Wife #1755
Beyond the Boardroom #1765
Thirty Day Affair #1785

Silhouette Nocturne

‡*Eternally* #4
‡*Nevermore* #10

*Three-Way Wager
**Summer of Secrets
‡The Guardians

MAUREEN CHILD

is a California native who loves to travel. Every chance they get, she and her husband are taking off on another research trip. The author of more than sixty books, Maureen loves a happy ending and still swears that she has the best job in the world. She lives in Southern California with her husband, two children, and a golden retriever with delusions of grandeur.

You can contact Maureen via her Web site: www.maureenchild.com

To Christie Ridgway, Susan Crosby,
Liz Bevarly, Anna DePalo and Susan Mallery.

Great writers all,
they made being a part of this series so much fun!

One

"Hunter," Nathan Barrister muttered as he stared at the mammoth wood-and-stone mansion on the shores of Lake Tahoe, "if you were here right now, I'd kill you for this."

Of course, Hunter Palmer wasn't there and Nathan couldn't kill the man who had once been his first—and best—friend, because he was already dead.

The ice around Nathan's heart thickened a little at the thought, but he used his long years of practice to ignore that tightening twinge. Regrets were a waste of time.

"As big a waste as the next month is going to be." He climbed out of his rental car and stepped into a mound of slush he hadn't even noticed.

With a disgusted sigh, he kicked the dirty snow off the polished toe of his shoe and told himself he should have listened to the clerk at the rental agency. She had tried to tell him that renting a four-wheel-drive car would make more sense than the sports car he preferred.

But who the hell expected snow in March for God's sake?

A wry grin curved his mouth briefly. *He* should have expected it. He'd grown up back east and should have remembered that snow could hit anytime, anywhere. Especially this high up in the mountains. But he'd spent so much time trying to forget his past, was it really surprising that even the *weather* had the ability to sneak up on him?

The air was cold and clean, and the sky was so blue it made his eyes ache. A sharp wind whipped through the surrounding pine trees, rustling the needles and sending patches of snow falling to the ground with muffled *plops*.

Nathan shivered and shrugged deeper into his brown leather jacket. He didn't want to be here at all, let alone for a solid month. He never stayed *anywhere* for more than a few days at a stretch. And being here made him think about things he hadn't allowed himself to remember in years.

Reluctantly, he headed for the front of the house, leaving his bags in the car for the moment. The crunch of his shoes on the ground was the only sound, as if the world were holding its breath. Great. Fifteen minutes here and his brain was already going off on tangents.

He shouldn't be here. He should still be in Tahiti at his family's hotel, going over the books, settling disputes, looking into expansion. And next month, he'd be in Barbados for a week and then Jamaica. Nathan moved fast, never giving himself a chance to settle. Never risking more than a few days in any one place.

Until now.

And if there had been any way at all of getting out of this, Nathan would have taken it. God knows, he'd tried to find a loophole in his friend's will. Something that would have allowed him to keep both his own sense of duty in place and his sanity intact. But even the Barrister family lawyers had assured him that the will was sealed nice and tight. Hunter Palmer had made sure that his friends would have no choice but to honor his wishes.

"You're enjoying this, aren't you?" Nathan whispered to his long-dead friend. And when the wind rattled the pine trees, damned if it didn't sound like laughter.

"Fine. I'm here. And I'll try to make the whole month," he muttered. Once he'd completed Hunter's last request, he hoped to hell his old friend would stop haunting his nightmares.

A long white envelope with his name scrawled across it was stuck to the heavy wood front door. Nathan took the short flight of snow-dusted wooden steps, stopped on the porch and tore the taped envelope free. Opening it, he found a key dangling from an ornate keychain and a single sheet of paper.

Hi, I'm your housekeeper, Meri. I'm very busy, so I'm not here at the moment, and chances are you won't be seeing me during your stay. But here's the key to the house. The kitchen is stocked and the town of Hunter's Landing is only twenty minutes away if you need anything else. I hope you and the others to follow enjoy your time here.

Without thinking, he crumpled the short note in his right hand and squeezed it hard.

The others.

In a flash of memory, Nathan went back ten years. Back to a time when he and his friends had called themselves the Seven Samurai. Foolish. But then, they'd been seniors at Harvard. They'd done four hard years together and come out the other side closer than brothers. They'd had their lives laying out in front of them like golden roads to success. He remembered the raucous evening with just a few too many beers when they'd vowed to build a house together and reunite in ten years. They'd each spend a month there and then gather in the seventh month to toast their inevitable achievements.

Yes, it was all supposed to work out that way. And then…

Nathan shook his head and let the past slide away. Jamming the key into the lock, he opened the door, stepped inside and stopped just inside the foyer. From there, he could see into a great room, with gleaming wood walls, a huge stone fireplace with a fire already ablaze in the hearth and lots of plush, comfortable-looking furniture.

As jail cells went, it was better than most, he supposed. He thought of the housekeeper and the nearby town and hoped to hell he wouldn't be bothered by a lot of people. Bad enough he was stuck here. He didn't need company on top of it.

He wasn't here to make friends. He was here to honor a friend he'd lost long ago.

An hour later, Keira Sanders grabbed the oversized basket off the passenger seat, leaped down from the driver's seat of her truck and slammed the door. Her boots slid around on the slushy ground but she dug in her heels and steadied herself. All she needed was to meet the first of Hunter Palmer's houseguests with dirty snow on her butt.

"Great first impression that would make," she murmured as she looked the house over.

It shone like a jewel in the gathering night. Light spilled from the tall windows to fall on the ground in golden spears. Smoke lifted from the stone chimney and twisted in the icy wind coming off the lake. Snow hugged the slanted roof and clung to the pines and aspens crowding the front yard. Winter tended to stick around this high up on the mountain, and she wouldn't have had it any other way.

There was something about the cold and the quiet hush of snow that had always felt…magical to Keira. In fact, at the moment, she'd like to be back in her cozy place in Hunter's Landing, sitting beside her own fire, with a glass of white wine and a good book.

Instead, she was here to greet the first of six men who would be spending thirty days each in the lakeside mansion. Nerves jumped in the pit of her stomach but Keira fought them down. This was too important—to the town of Hunter's Landing and to her, personally.

Just two weeks ago, she'd received a very legal letter from the estate of a man named Hunter Palmer. In the letter, the late Mr. Palmer's attorney had explained the unusual bequest.

Over the next six months, six different men would be arriving in the town of Hunter's Landing, to spend thirty days in this gorgeous mansion. If each of the men stayed for the entire month, at the end of the six-month period twenty million dollars would be donated to charity—a large chunk of which would belong to Hunter's Landing—and the house itself would be donated to the town as a vacation home for recovering cancer patients.

Keira took another deep breath to settle the last of her nerves. As the mayor of Hunter's Landing, it was her job to make sure each of the six men held to the stipulations of Hunter Palmer's will. She couldn't afford for her small town to miss out on a windfall that would allow them to have a spanking-new clinic and a new jail and courthouse and…

Her head was spinning as she smiled to herself. She tightened her grip on the basket and checked to make sure the lid was latched down. Tugging at the lapels of her black jacket, she straightened her shoulders, plastered a smile on her face and prepared to meet the first of the men who could mean so much to Hunter's Landing.

She was good with people. Always had been. And now, with so much riding on the next six months, she was more determined than ever that everything go right. Not only would she ensure that each of the six men would stay his entire thirty days at the lakeside lodge, she was going to make sure they knew how much this all meant to her hometown.

With that thought firmly in mind, she gulped a deep breath of frosty air and headed for the front door. Her boots crunched in the snow but, when she hit a patch of ice, her feet slid wildly. "Oh, no."

Eyes wide, she held tightly to the basket and swung her arms in a desperate attempt to regain her balance. But her feet couldn't find purchase and as she tipped and swayed, she knew she was going to lose both her balance and her dignity.

"Ow!" she shouted when she hit the ground, landing so hard on her butt that her teeth rattled. The basket tipped to one side and she groaned, hoping that the contents were tightly sealed. "Well, isn't this perfect."

The front door flew open and light spilled over her. She blinked up at the man silhouetted in the doorway. Oh, man. This so wasn't how she'd planned to meet Nathan Barrister.

"Who're you?" he demanded, making no move to come down the steps to help her up.

"I'm fine, thanks for your concern," she said, wincing as icy, wet cold seeped through the seat of her jeans. So much for first impressions. Maybe she should crawl back to her truck and start all over.

"If you're thinking of suing, you should know I don't own this property," he said.

"Wow." For a moment, Keira forgot all about getting up—forgot all about the fact that this man and five others just like him could mean a windfall for Hunter's Landing—and just sat there, staring at him in amazement. "You're really a jerk, aren't you?"

"I beg your pardon?"

"Did I say that out loud?"

"Yes."

"Sorry." And she was. Sort of. For heaven's sake, none of this was going as planned.

"Are you injured?"

"Only my pride," she admitted, though her behind hurt like hell and the melting ice beneath her wasn't helping the situation any. Still, might as well make the best of the situation. She raised one hand and waved it. "A little help here?"

He muttered something she didn't catch and, considering his attitude so far, she considered that a good thing. But he came down the steps carefully, grabbed her hand and pulled her to her feet in one quick motion.

His fingers on hers felt warm and strong and…good. Okay, she hadn't expected that. He dropped her hand as if he'd been burned, and she wondered if he'd felt that small zap of something hot and interesting when they touched.

She brushed off the seat of her pants while she looked up at him. For some reason she'd expected him to be an older man. But he wasn't. Tall and lean, he had broad shoulders, a narrow waist and long legs. Considering how easily he'd plucked her off the ice, he was strong, too. Not that she was heavy or anything, but she certainly wasn't one of those stick-figure types of women that were so popular these days.

Ordinarily, a man like him was more than enough to make her heart go pitty-pat. However, the scowl on his truly gorgeous face was enough to make even Keira rethink her attraction. His black hair was stylishly cut to just above his collar. His blue eyes were narrowed on her suspiciously, and his hard jaw was clenched. And his full mouth was tightened into a grim slash across his face, letting her know without a doubt just how welcome she wasn't.

"Wow. Are you really in a bad mood or is it just me?"

He blew out a breath. "Whoever you are," he said, his voice a low rumble that seemed to dip all the way inside her to start up a slow fire, "I didn't invite you here. And I'm not interested in meeting my neighbors."

"Good," Keira said, grinning at his obvious irritation, "because you don't have any. The nearest house on the lake is a couple miles north."

He frowned at her. "Then who are you?"

"Keira Sanders," she said, holding out one hand and leaving it there until rudimentary good manners forced him to take it in his.

Again, there was the nice little buzz of connection when his skin met hers. Did he feel it? If so, he wasn't real pleased about it. Keira, on the other hand, was enjoying the sensation. It had been a really long time since she'd felt the slightest attraction for anyone. Purposely. "Been there, done that" sort of summed up her feelings about romance.

But she had to admit, it was really nice to feel that sizzle.

Still shaking his hand, she smiled up into his scowl. Gorgeous, but crabby. Well, she'd dealt with irritable people before, and there was just no way she was going to let his bad attitude affect Hunter's Landing's chances at getting money that would be a godsend to the small town. "I'm the mayor of Hunter's Landing and I'm here to welcome you."

"That's not necessary," he said and dropped her hand.

"It's our pleasure," she said, hanging on to her good cheer by her fingernails as she turned to pluck the basket out of the snow. "And," she continued as she walked past him, headed toward the front door, "I've brought you a welcome basket, courtesy of the Hunter's Landing Chamber of Commerce."

"If you don't mind," he countered, following after her quickly.

"Not at all," Keira said, walking into the house and stopping just inside the foyer. "I confess, I've been dying to see the inside of this place ever since they started building it last year."

It took a moment or two, but she heard him come in behind her and close the door with an exasperated sigh. He was not just crabby, but very crabby, apparently.

But that was okay. She'd win him over. She had to. She had to make sure that he and the five others who would come after him here would complete the terms of the will that would so benefit her hometown.

"Ms. Sanders…"

"Call me Keira," she said and turned to give him a quick glance and smile.

"Fine. Keira." He shoved both hands into the pockets of his slacks and rocked back on his heels.

He *really* didn't want her there.

"Don't worry," she said, stepping through the arched doorway into the great room, "I won't stay long. I only wanted to welcome you, let you know that you're not alone here."

"I prefer alone," he said flatly and she stopped halfway across the room and turned to look at him, still standing in the foyer.

"Now, why is that?" she wondered aloud.

His features tightened even further, until he looked as though he'd been carved from stone. Not really a people person, Keira decided, then shrugged.

"Anyway," she said loudly, setting the basket down atop a hand-carved coffee table that probably cost more than her monthly house payment. "I've got a few goodies here to make your stay more comfortable."

"I'm sure I'll be fine."

She ignored him and started rooting through the basket, pulling items out, one after the other, with a brief description of each. "Here's a certificate good for free coffee and freshly made doughnuts every morning at the diner. And a jar of homemade jam—Margie Fontenot, the late mayor's widow, makes the best jam in the state. A bottle of wine from Stan's Liquor Stop, fresh bread from the bakery, a bag of ground Jamaican coffee beans—" she stopped to sniff the bag and sighed at the aroma, then continued "—there's a jar filled with the best marinara you've ever tasted, from Clearwater's restaurant—you really should get over there for dinner while you're here. The outside dining area overlooks the lake and there's no better place to catch a gorgeous sunset—"

"Ms. Sanders…"

"Keira," she reminded him.

"Keira, then. If you don't mind—"

"And," she went on as if he hadn't spoken, "there are a few more goodies in here, but I'll let you discover them on your own."

"Thank you."

"Now," she said, turning to face him from across the room, "is there anything else I can do to help make your stay more interesting?"

"Leave?" he asked.

Keira shook her head at him, as if she were sorely disappointed. Wandering the great room, she ran her fingers along the deeply carved mantel over the fireplace and, just for a second or two, enjoyed the heat pouring from the hearth. Her gaze swept the rest of the room and lingered on the view of the lake out of the floor-to-ceiling windows. The moon was just beginning its climb across the sky, and the water shimmered with a breath of light as if waiting for the show to start.

She gave herself a moment or two to calm the flash of irritation inside her. Wouldn't do to insult the man whose very presence could mean so much to her town. But at the same time, she wondered why he was being so nasty. By the time she'd centered herself and turned her gaze back to him, *still* standing in the foyer as if he could force her to leave by simply not welcoming her in, she was wondering something else.

Why did he intrigue her so much when his rudeness should have put her off immediately?

And how was she going to make this man connect with Hunter's Landing and make a commitment to see this through when he so obviously wanted nothing to do with her or the town?

Two

Nathan had had enough.

He'd been at the lakeside mansion for a little over an hour and already he had an uninvited guest.

Plus, Keira Sanders seemed to be oblivious to insults and clearly didn't care that she was very obviously not wanted.

His gaze swept her up and down more thoroughly than he had when he'd first found her sitting in the snow. Her jeans were faded and hugged her long legs like a second skin. Her long-sleeved black sweater came down to her thighs and, ridiculously enough, made her figure look more exposed than hidden. Maybe it was the way the soft-looking fabric clung to her curves, but whatever the reason, Nathan could appreciate the view even while wishing she were anywhere but there.

Her shoulder-length, reddish-blond hair hung loose in waves that seemed to dance around her animated face whenever she moved—which was often. He'd never seen a more mobile woman. It was as if she couldn't bear standing still. She was wandering the great room, her fingers touching, stroking, everything as she passed and he couldn't help wondering what those fingers would feel like touching *him*.

Yet as soon as that thought hit his clearly fevered brain, he knew he had to get her the hell out of the house. He wasn't interested in a monthlong fling. That was more commitment than he'd given to any woman he'd known in the last ten years.

Best to just get her out of the house now. And if that meant being even ruder than he had been already, fine.

"Thank you for coming," he said, waiting until she gave up examining the bookshelves to look at him again, "but if you don't mind, I'd like you to leave."

There. A man couldn't be any more plainspoken than that.

"Wow," she said softly, her green eyes sparkling in reflected light from the fire, "nobody ever taught you how to treat your guests?"

He swallowed hard and pushed away the thought of just how horrified his grandmother would have been at his blatant rudeness. "You're not a guest," he said tightly, reminding her as well as himself. "You're an intruder."

She actually laughed at him. "But I'm an intruder who brought you gifts!"

Nathan finally left the foyer, since it seemed clear that standing beside the door wasn't going to be enough to convince her to step through it. He'd never met

anyone else quite like her. She seemed impervious to
rudeness, just rolling right along with a cheerful attitude
that must, he thought, really annoy the hell out of people
who knew her well.

"Look," Nathan said, walking across the polished
floor toward her. "I've tried to be polite."

She blinked at him and her smile widened. "Really?
That was trying?"

Frowning, he ignored the jab and said, "I appreciate
the gifts. Thank you for taking the time to come out
here. But I would really prefer to be *alone.*"

"Oh, I'm sure you want to settle in," she said, waving
one hand at him, blithely ignoring his attempt to get rid
of her. "And I won't stay much longer, I swear."

Hope to cling to.

"I only wanted to let you know that Hunter's Landing
is ready to help you and the other men who will be
staying here in any way we can." She wandered to the
big-screen TV, picked up the remote and studied it for
a second or two.

If she turned the damn thing on, she might never
leave. Nathan walked to her side, took the remote and
set it down on a nearby table. She shrugged, walked to
the windows overlooking the lake and stood staring
through the glass as if mesmerized.

He watched her and couldn't help feeling a little
mesmerized himself. The fall of her hair on her shoulders. The curve of her behind. The defiant tilt to her
chin. She turned to look at him and her wide, shining
eyes fixed on him with a slam of power he didn't want
to think about.

"You'll only be here a month," she said quietly, "and

maybe you don't realize just how important your stay and the others' are to Hunter's Landing."

Nathan sighed and resigned himself to at least a few more minutes of conversation. It seemed plain that Keira Sanders wasn't going to leave until she was good and ready. "I know about what your town stands to inherit from the estate."

"But you can't know what it means to us," she insisted, half turning to lean one shoulder against the cold glass. "With that influx of cash, we can build a new courthouse, expand our clinic…" Her voice trailed off and she smiled as if already seeing the changes that would happen to her town.

"And speaking of the clinic," she said quickly, straightening up and walking toward him. "I want to invite you to the town potluck dinner tomorrow night. We're raising money to get the expansion started and—"

"But you'll have the inheritance—"

"Can't count on that until it's reality, can we?" she pointed out, neatly cutting him off before he could finish his sentence. "Anyway, our clinic is good, but it's not nearly big enough. Of course, there's a terrific hospital in Lake Tahoe, but that's a long drive, especially in the winter snow. We need to be able to take care of our own citizens right here and, with the potluck dinner, all the money collected will go directly into the fund for…"

She was talking so fast Nathan's ears were buzzing. He had no interest in going to her community fundraiser and he suspected that she didn't really want him there, either. What she wanted was a donation. Wasn't that what everyone wanted from him in the end?

With the Barrister family fortune behind him, Nathan

had long ago accepted that he was seen first as a bankbook and second as a man. Which suited him fine. He didn't want friends. Didn't want a lover or a wife. What he wanted was to be left alone.

And he suddenly knew just the way to hurry Keira Sanders out the door: Give her what she wanted. What she'd really come for. While she continued to talk in nearly a stream of consciousness while hardly pausing for breath, he stalked across the room to where he'd dropped his briefcase on one of the overstuffed, burgundy leather chairs. Quickly, he opened it, grabbed his black leather checkbook and flicked his ballpoint pen.

Shaking his head, he wrote a check made out to Hunter's Landing, and then tore it from the pad and walked back to where Keira was still smiling and outlining the plans she had for her little town.

"So you see, it would be a great chance for you to meet everyone in town. Nice for you to see the place you'll be living for the next month and maybe it will help you see how important it is to us that you and your friends complete the stipulations of Mr. Palmer's will." She finally took a breath. "If it's okay with you, I'll pick you up tomorrow about six and drive you to the potluck myself. I can take you on a tour of the lake if you'd like too and—"

"Please," Nathan said, interrupting her when it became obvious it would be the only way to keep her quiet. He held out the check and waited until she'd taken it, a question in her beautiful eyes. "Accept this contribution to your clinic fund."

"Oh," she said, "that's very generous of you but—" She stopped, glanced down at the check and Nathan actually *saw* all the blood drain from her face. She went absolutely white and her hand holding the check trembled. "I…I…you…"

Her mouth opened and closed, she gulped noisily and wheezed in a breath. "Oh. My. God."

"Are you all right?" Nathan reached for her, grabbed her upper arm and felt the tremors that were racing through her body.

She raised her gaze to his, waved the check in a tight fist and swallowed hard a time or two before trying to speak. Apparently, he'd finally found the way to make her speechless.

"Are you *serious* about this?"

"The check?"

"The *amount*," she said harshly, then added, "I've got to sit down."

And she did.

Right there on the floor.

She pulled her arm free of his grasp and folded up on herself. Leaning her head back against the closest chair, she looked up at him in stunned amazement. "I can't believe you—"

"It's just a donation," he said.

"Of *five hundred thousand dollars*," she pointed out.

"If you don't want it…"

"Oh, no!" She folded the check and stretched out her right leg so she could stuff it into her jeans pocket. Then she patted it carefully and gave him a grin. "We want it. And we thank you. I mean, the whole *town* is going to want to thank you. This is just wonderful. Completely generous. I don't know what to say, really—"

"And yet you keep trying," Nathan said, feeling

oddly embarrassed the longer she went on about a simple donation.

"Wow. My head's still spinning. In a good way," she insisted, then raised one hand toward him. "A little help here?"

Nathan sighed, reached for her hand and, in one quick move, pulled her to her feet. She flew off the floor and slammed into his chest with a *whoosh* of air pushed from her lungs. His hands dropped to her waist to steady her and, for a quick moment, he considered kissing her.

Which surprised the hell out of him.

Keira Sanders wasn't the kind of woman who usually attracted him. For one, she was too damn talkative. He liked a woman who appreciated a good silence. And she was short. He liked tall women. And he preferred brunettes. And blue eyes.

Yet, as she looked at him, her green eyes seemed to pull at him, drawing him in, tugging him closer than he wanted to be.

With her breasts smashed up against his broad chest, Keira felt a rush of something hot and needy and completely unexpected. The man was as closed-off as a dead-end road, and yet there was something about him that made her want to reach up, wrap her arms around his neck and pull his head down for a long, lingering kiss.

And it *wasn't* the huge check that was sitting in her pocket like a red-hot coal.

"You're a very surprising man," she finally said when she was pretty sure she could speak without her voice breaking.

His hands dropped from her waist and he stepped back so quickly that her shaky balance made her wobble unsteadily before she found stability again.

"It's just a check."

"It's more than that," she assured him. God, she couldn't wait to show his donation to the town council. Eva Callahan would probably keel over in a dead faint. "You have no idea what this means to our town."

"You're welcome," he said tightly. "Now, if you don't mind, I have some work I have to get to."

"No you don't," she said, smiling.

"I'm sorry?"

"You don't have any work," Keira said, tipping her head to one side to study him, as if getting a different perspective might help understand why such a deliberately solitary man could give away so much money without even pausing to think about it. "You just want me to go."

"Yes." His frown deepened. "I believe I already mentioned that."

"So you did." She patted the check in her pocket, swung her hair back from her face and gave him a smile. "And I'm going to oblige you."

A flicker of something like acceptance shot across his eyes, and Keira wondered about that for a second or two. But then his features evened out into a mask of granite that no amount of staring at would ever decipher.

"Okay then," she said, starting for the front door, only half surprised when he made no move to follow her. He'd seemed so anxious to get rid of her, she'd just assumed that he'd show her out once he had the chance. But when she turned to glance back at him, he was standing where she'd left him.

Alone, in front of the vast windows overlooking the lake. Behind him, the water silvered under the rising moon and the star-swept sky seemed to stretch on forever. Something inside her wanted to go back to him. To somehow make him less *solitary*.

But she knew he wouldn't welcome it.

For whatever reason, Nathan Barrister had become a man so used to solitude he didn't want or expect anything to change.

Well, Keira wasn't going to allow him to get away with an anonymous donation. She was going to make sure the town got the chance to thank him properly for what he had done for them with a click of a pen.

Whether he liked it or not, Keira was going to drag Nathan into the heart of Hunter's Landing.

By the next evening, Keira was running on adrenaline. She'd hardly been able to sleep the night before; memories of Nathan Barrister and the feel of his hands on her had kept her tossing and turning through some pretty detailed fantasies that kept playing through her mind.

Ridiculous, really. She knew the man would be here for only a month. She knew he wasn't interested—he'd made *that* plain enough every time he looked at her. But, for some reason, her body hadn't gotten the message.

She felt hot and itchy and…way more needy than she'd like to admit.

Apparently it had been way too long since she'd had a man in her life. But then, the last man she'd been interested in had made such a mess of her world that she'd pretty much sworn off the Y chromosome.

Then grumpy, rich and gorgeous Nathan Barrister,

rolled into her life and made her start rethinking a few things. Not a good idea.

She spun her straw through her glass of iced tea and watched idly as ice cubes rattled against the sides of the glass. It felt good to sit down. She'd been running all day, first calling an emergency meeting of the town council so she could tell them about Nathan's donation. And, she smiled as she remembered, Eva Callahan had behaved as expected, slumping into a chair and waving a stack of papers at her face to stave off a faint.

Once the meeting was over she'd had to take care of a few other things, like depositing that check, talking to the contractor about the renovations to the clinic, settling a parking dispute between Harry's Hardware and Frannie's Fabrics and finally, coming here to the Lakeside Diner.

Being mayor of a small town was exhausting, and it was really hardly more than an honorary office. Her duties consisted mainly of presiding over town council meetings once a month, playing referee to adults old enough to solve their own problems and trying to raise money for civic projects. And yet, she seemed to always be busy. She didn't have a clue how the mayors of big cities managed to have a life at all.

But then, Keira thought, isn't that the way she wanted it? Keeping busy gave her too little time to think about how her life had turned out so differently from what she'd expected. She picked a French fry off her plate and popped it into her mouth. Chewing, she glanced around the crowded diner and took a deep breath. Here, no matter what else was going on in her life, Keira could find comfort.

The Lakeside Diner was a tiny coffee shop and more or less a touchstone in Keira's life, the one constant she'd always been able to count on. Her parents had owned and operated the diner before her and she herself had started working here, clearing tables, when she was twelve.

Then, when her parents died, Keira had taken over, because there was her younger sister, Kelly, to provide for. Now, she had a manager to take care of the day-to-day running of the diner, but when she needed a place to sit and recharge, she always came here.

The red Naugahyde booths were familiar, as was the gleaming wood counter and the glass covered cake and pie dishes, the records in the jukebox her father had loved hadn't been changed in twenty years. Memories crowded thick in this diner. She closed her eyes and could almost see her dad behind the stove, grinning out at her mom running the cash register.

This diner—like Hunter's Landing—was *home.*

"Hey, Keira. Can I see it?"

She opened her eyes, startled as an older woman slid onto the bench seat opposite her. Sallye Carberry grinned, and held out one hand dotted with silver rings.

"See what?" Keira asked.

"The check, of course," Sallye prompted. "Everyone in town is talking about it. Margie Fontenot told me that she'd never seen anything quite so pretty as all those zeros. I just wanted an up close peek at it."

"Sorry, Sallye," Keira said, taking a sip of her tea. "Already deposited it."

"Well, darn." The older woman slumped back against the seat and huffed out a disappointed breath that waved the curl of bangs on her forehead. "That's a bummer."

Keira laughed.

Sallye waved one beringed hand. "That's okay, I'll settle for meeting the man himself. I hear he's a real looker. He *is* coming to the potluck so we can all get a look at him—I mean thank him—isn't he?"

There was the question.

She knew damn well Nathan wouldn't want anything to do with the town or their potluck dinner. She knew he didn't want their thanks and was pretty sure he wouldn't want to see her again any time soon. So anyone with a grain of sense would keep her distance, right?

The last thing she should do was go back to the lakeside mansion to see a man who wanted nothing to do with her.

And yet…

Keira checked her silver wristwatch, saw she had a couple of hours until six and took one last sip of her tea. Sliding from the booth, she looked down at her late mother's best friend and nodded. "He'll be there," she said firmly.

Three

Nathan felt like a prisoner.

And damn it, he shouldn't.

He *preferred* being alone.

But this kind of alone was too damned quiet.

He stepped out onto the deck overlooking Lake Tahoe and let the cold wind buffet him. His hair lifted in the icy breeze, and he narrowed his eyes as he stared out over a snowy landscape. Silence pounded at him. Even the soft sigh of the lake water slapping against the deck pilings seemed overly loud in the eerie stillness.

The problem was, Nathan thought, he wasn't used to this kind of alone. Other people considered him a recluse but, even in his insular world, there was more…interaction.

He traveled constantly, moving from one of his

family's hotels to the next. And on those trips he dealt with room service personnel, hotel managers, maids, waiters, the occasional guest. No matter how he tried to avoid contact with people, there were always some who he was forced to speak to.

Until now.

The plain truth was he hated being completely alone even more than he hated being in a crowd.

His fists tightened on the varnished wood railing until he wouldn't have been surprised to see the imprint of his fingers digging into the wood. He was used to people jumping when he spoke. To his employees practically doing backflips to accommodate his wishes. He liked dropping in on his favorite casino in Monte Carlo and spending the night with whatever blonde, brunette or redhead was the most convenient. He liked the sounds of champagne bottles popping and crystal clinking, and the muted sound of sophisticated laughter. He was accustomed to picking up a phone and ordering a meal. To calling his pilot to get his jet ready to leave at a moment's notice.

Yet now he knew he couldn't go anywhere.

And that was the real irritant chewing at him. Nathan hadn't stayed in any one place for more than three or four days since he was a kid. Which was exactly how he wanted it. Knowing that he was *trapped* on top of this damned mountain for a damned *month* was enough to make him want to call his pilot now.

Why he didn't was a mystery to him.

"Hunter, you really owe me big time," he said and didn't know whether to look toward heaven or hell as he uttered the words.

Hunter Palmer had been a good guy, but reaching out from beyond the grave to put Nathan through this should have earned him a seat in hell.

"Why did I come here in the first place?" he whispered, asking himself the question and knowing he didn't have an answer.

Old loyalties was not a good enough reason.

It has been ten years since Hunter had died. Ten years since Nathan had even thought of those days, of the friend he'd lost too young. Of the five others who had been such a huge part of his life. He'd moved on. Built his world just the way he wanted it and didn't give a damn what anyone else had to say about it. That pledge the Samurai had made to one another? It seemed to come from another lifetime.

He thought briefly of the framed photos of the Seven Samurai, as they'd called themselves back then, hanging here in the upstairs hall. Every time he passed them, he deliberately looked away. Studying the past was for archaeologists. Not barristers. He didn't owe Hunter or any of the others anything. College friendships were routinely left behind as life continued on. So why in hell was he here?

A bird skimmed the water's surface, its wings stretched wide, its shadow moving on the lake as if it had a life of its own. "And even the damn bird is freer than I am."

Pushing away from the rail, he turned his back on the expansive view of nature's beauty and walked back into what he was already considering his cell.

He glanced at the television, then rejected the idea of turning it on. There were plenty of books to read, and even a state-of-the-art office loft upstairs but he couldn't imagine sitting still long enough to truly accomplish anything, at the moment, all he could do was prowl. He could take a walk, but he might just keep on walking, right down the mountain to the airport where his private Gulfstream waited for him.

"I'm never gonna make the whole damn month," he muttered, shoving one hand through his hair and turning toward the table where his laptop sat open.

He took a seat, hit a few keys and checked his e-mail as soon as the Internet connection came through. Two new letters were there, one each from the managers of the London and Tokyo Barrister hotels.

Once he'd dealt with their questions about his schedule, Nathan was at a loss again. There was only so much work he could do long-distance. After all, if he wasn't there in person, he couldn't scowl at his employees.

When the doorbell rang, he jumped to his feet. This is what he'd come to, then. Grateful for an interruption. For someone—anyone—to interrupt the silence that continued to claw at him. He closed the laptop and stalked across the great room to the front door.

When he opened the door, he said, "I should have guessed it would be you."

Keira grinned, slipped past him into the house and then turned to look at him. "You're going to need a coat."

Nathan closed the door and didn't admit even to himself that he was glad to see her. As annoying as she was, she was, at least, another voice in this damned quiet.

"I'm warm enough, thanks."

"No, I mean, the potluck is outside so you'll really need a coat." She turned again and walked into the great room as if she belonged there. Her voice echoed in the high-ceilinged room and her footsteps sounded like a heartbeat. "We could have held the dinner at the court-house, but it's a little cramped and the band said it would be easier to set up outside."

"The band?"

"Uh-huh," she said, looking around as if she hadn't just seen the place the day before, "it's a local group. Super Leo. They play mostly rock but they'll take requests, too, and they're good guys. They all grew up here."

"Fascinating," Nathan said, moving to the edge of the foyer, leaning one shoulder against the wall and crossing one foot over the other as he watched her move. Damn, the woman looked good.

It was the solitude getting to him. The only explanation why he was interested in a short, mouthy redhead when ordinarily, he never would have looked at her twice. The fact that he'd only been "enjoying" this solitude for a day didn't really matter.

"The town council approved new lights for this year, so the square will be bright as day with plenty of room for dancing. When I left they were already setting the food out on the tables and the band was tuning up, so we really should get going if you don't want to miss anything."

"Miss anything?" Nathan shook his head. "I told you yesterday that I had no interest in going to your town party or whatever."

"Well, I didn't think you *meant* it."

"Why not?"

"Who wouldn't want to go to a party?"

"Me." Now, if the party were in St. Tropez, or Gstaad, he'd be right there. But a small-town party in the middle of Nowhere, U.S.A.? No, thanks.

She stared at him as if he'd just grown another

head. Then she shrugged and went on as if he hadn't said a word.

"The town council was incredibly grateful for your donation."

"You told them?" An uncomfortable itch settled between his shoulder blades. He didn't mind donating money. It was simply a part of who he was. But he preferred anonymity. He didn't want gratitude. He just wanted to be left alone.

But even as he thought this, he realized that he'd been complaining about the solitude just a minute before.

"Of course I told them," she said, picking up a throw pillow from the couch and fluffing it before she dropped it back into place. "Who am I, Santa? Dropping money into the town coffers without an explanation? I don't think so. They all want to meet you, to thank you for your generosity."

"Not necessary."

"Oh, but it really is," she said and reached down to straighten a stack of magazines strewn across the coffee table. "If you don't come to the potluck so everyone can meet you…"

"Yeah?"

She shrugged. "Then I guess everyone will just have to come to *you*."

Nathan sighed. She was blackmailing him into attending her damned town function. And doing a pretty good job of it, too. If he didn't go, he had no doubt that she'd lead droves of citizens up the mountain to intrude on the lodge. He'd be hip-deep in people before he knew it.

"Extortion?"

"Let's call it judicial negotiations."

"And if I go to the party, you'll leave me alone."

She held up one hand like a Girl Scout salute and said, "I so solemnly swear."

"I don't believe you."

"Gee, attractive, crabby *and* smart."

A smile twitched at his mouth, but he fought it into submission. No point in encouraging her any.

"Fine. I'll go."

"Wow," she said, patting her hand over her heart, "I'm all excited."

Her green eyes were shining and a smile curved her tantalizing mouth. The gray sweater she wore beneath a black leather jacket outlined the swell of her breasts, and her faded jeans and battered boots made her look too tempting to a man who was going to be trapped on a damn mountaintop for a month.

So Nathan got a grip on his hormonal overdrive and turned to the hall closet. He opened it, snatched out his brown leather jacket and pulled it on over his dark green cashmere sweater.

A few minutes ago, he'd been complaining that he was too alone. Now, he was going to a block party, of all things.

Be careful what you wish for.

Keira sneaked glances at him as she drove down the mountain. His profile was enough to make her heart stutter and when he turned his head to look at her, she almost drove into a tree.

"Whoops." She over-straightened and her snow tires slipped a little on an icy patch of road.

"Was this a ploy to get me on the road long enough to kill me?"

"Everything's fine," she said, tightening her grip on the wheel. "But would you like to take a look around before we head into town?"

"No, thanks." He checked the gold watch on his left wrist. "I can only spare an hour or two."

"Why?"

"Because."

"Ah. Good reason." Keira smiled and followed the curve of the road. There was a steep drop-off beyond the white barrier and Nathan glanced down into the abyss.

"Look," he said, "I'm only coming to this party to avoid the alternative."

"Don't worry, you'll be glad you came."

"Why do you care if I attend this party or not?"

"Why?" She risked another glance at him as soon as the road straightened, then turned her gaze ahead again. "You and the others who'll stay at the lodge after you are doing something tremendous for our town. Why wouldn't we want to thank you for that?"

He shifted uncomfortably on the truck seat. "I can't speak for the others, but I'm not doing this for you or your town."

"Then why?"

His mouth flattened into a grim line. "It's not important."

"But it's important enough for you to come here. To stay for a month?"

Still scowling, he said, "I'm here. As to the month… I don't know."

A small spear of panic jolted through Keira at the thought that he might leave. If he did, then, according to the terms of the will she'd read, the town of Hunter's

Landing would get nothing and the lakeside mansion would be sold.

She couldn't let that happen.

She *had* to convince Nathan Barrister to stay for the whole month. And maybe the best way to do that was to show him the town he and his friends were going to help. To let him see firsthand what a difference a month of his time could make to all of them.

But if he really wanted to go, how could she make him stay?

"But you agreed to the month."

"I did," he said, and she sensed, more than saw, him shrug his broad shoulders. "But I don't know that it's feasible. I have businesses to watch over. Places I'm supposed to be."

Already he was making mental excuses. Giving himself an out. Looking for a way to escape the terms of the will. The panic Keira's heart felt a moment ago jumped into hyperactive life and did a quick two step in the pit of her stomach. Did he believe that by making that incredibly generous donation he didn't have to complete the terms of the will?

"You wouldn't really leave soon, would you?"

He shifted in his seat and the leather creaked as he moved. "If you're looking for guarantees, I can't give them to you."

"But you agreed to the terms."

"Yes."

"So your word's not worth much?"

He frowned at her. "Is insulting me your grand plan to get me to cooperate? If so, it's a bad idea."

"Probably." She sighed and took the final turn down

the mountain road. Just a half mile ahead was Hunter's Landing, where her friends and neighbors were celebrating and planning the changes that would be coming at the end of six months.

She wondered how happy they'd all be to meet Nathan Barrister if they knew just how close he was to ruining those plans.

Pulling the car off to the side of the road, Keira threw the gearshift into park, yanked up the emergency brake and turned in her seat to look at him head-on.

"Problem?" he asked.

"You could say so," she said. In the darkening light, his pale blue eyes shone like chips of ice—and were just as welcoming. "This might not mean much to you," she said, "but your staying here for the entire month can mean a huge difference to the people here."

"I didn't say I was leaving," he pointed out.

"You didn't say you were staying, either," she countered.

"I am for right now," he said.

"That's supposed to make me feel better? Right now?"

"It's all I can give you."

Keira wanted to grab him and shake him, but she knew that wouldn't do any good. He was so closed-off, so shut down from anything other than his own feelings, she'd need a hammer to pound home her point. Tempting, but probably not logical.

"You've been here only one day. Give it a chance. Give *us* a chance."

He looked at her in the waning light and, just for a second, Keira thought those eyes of his warmed a little.

But she was probably mistaken since an instant later, they were cool and distant again.

"If you do," she added, "who knows, you might just like it here."

One dark eyebrow rose. "I'm not expecting to like it."

"Well," she said, smiling as she turned to shift the car into gear again and head into town, "surprises happen every day."

"Whether I stay or go is really none of your business." His tone clearly stated that was the end of the discussion.

Well, Keira wasn't sure who he was used to dealing with, but she wasn't about to back down under that king-to-peasant attitude.

"That's where you're wrong, Nathan." She paused and threw him a smile designed to either put him at ease or worry him half to death. "You don't mind if I call you Nathan, right? Well, Nathan, it *is* my business to see that you stay here. As mayor, I can't let you walk away from something that will mean so much to us."

He studied her for a long minute. She felt his gaze on her and forced herself to keep her own gaze focused on the road ahead of her. As they got closer to town, she heard the still-distant sounds of the band playing and steeled herself for whatever he was going to say next.

"Just so you know, Keira, if I decide to go, there's no way you'll be able to stop me."

She took the last turn in the road and saw Hunter's Landing spilling out ahead of her. Party lights were strung across the street, tiny blazes of white in the gathering darkness. People crowded the whole area, and a few couples had already started dancing.

Her heart swelled with love for the place and the

people she'd grown up with. Determination filled her as she turned to glance at the man beside her. She smiled and said, "Nathan, never issue a challenge like that to me. You'll lose every time."

They were swept into the party the moment she parked the truck, and Keira watched with some amusement as Nathan was dragged unwillingly into the center of things. The man was so stiff, so aloof, he stood out from the crowd like an ostrich in a chicken coop.

With the band's music pouring over them in a continuous wave of sound, Keira stood to one side and watched Nathan's features tighten as a few of the older men gathered around him to give Nathan some advice on fly-fishing.

The devil inside her told Keira to leave him to it. To let him be surrounded by the townspeople she'd so wanted him to meet. But a rational voice in the back of her mind drowned out that little devil by pointing out that if he *hated* it here, he'd have little reason to stay for the month to insure the town's bequest.

So she walked up to the group of men, smiled and said, "Sorry, guys, but I'm going to steal Nathan away for a dance."

"Aw, now, Keira, we're just telling him about the best spots in the Truckee River for fishing," one of them argued.

"And it was fascinating," Nathan said, dropping one arm around Keira's shoulders and dragging her in close to his side, as if afraid she'd change her mind and leave him there for more fishing advice. "But if you'll excuse me, gentlemen, I did promise the lady a dance."

Keira hid her smile and told herself that the warmth of Nathan's arm around her had more to do with body heat than sexual pull. Although she wasn't easily convinced, since parts of her that hadn't been hot in a very long time were suddenly smoking with sizzle and warmth.

When they moved away from the crowd toward the dance floor, Nathan bent his head and muttered, "I don't know whether to thank you for rescuing me or throttle you for bringing me here in the first place."

His voice was nearly lost under the slam of sound, so Keira leaned in closer to make sure he heard her response. "But you looked like you were having so much fun."

"I don't fish," he muttered.

"Maybe not," she pointed out, "but thanks to Sam Dover and the others, you could now if you wanted to."

He stopped and, since his arm was still wrapped around her shoulder, she did a quick stop too and slammed into his side.

"You're enjoying this, aren't you?"

"Would it be wrong to say yes?"

He frowned down at her. "I don't think I've ever met anyone like you before."

"Nathan! A compliment?"

"I'm not sure that's how I meant it."

She grinned. "That's how I'm taking it."

"Big surprise."

Keira wasn't fooled. There was a twitch at the corner of his way-too-kissable mouth that told her he was fighting the urge to smile. In the last day or so, she'd noticed he fought down smiling a lot. And she wondered why.

"So," she asked, "are you really going to dance with me?"

He sighed. "If I don't, are you going to sic the fishermen on me again?"

She lifted her arms into the dance-with-me position and said, "Nothing wrong with a good threat."

Four

The music slowed down into as close as a rock band could get to a romantic ballad, and Nathan reached for Keira. The instant his arm went around her waist, he felt a charge of something that jolted him from the soles of his feet straight up through the top of his head.

She smiled at him and he knew she'd felt it, too.

Her right hand felt small in his and the featherlight weight of her left hand seemed to be branding his shoulder. The air was icy and the street was crowded with people, yet he felt as if he and Keira were alone in the tropics, heat pouring through them with enough intensity to kindle a white-hot flame.

"What're you thinking?" she asked as he steered her around the makeshift dance floor in the middle of town.

"I don't think I'll tell you," he said and deliberately

raised his gaze from the sparkling beauty of her green eyes. "I have a feeling you'd find a way to use it against me."

"Oh, you're a sharp businessman, aren't you?" she asked, and suppressed laughter colored her voice.

He risked a glance down at her and found that the power in her gaze hadn't lessened a bit. "You've already blackmailed me *once*," he reminded her.

"For a good cause," she pointed out.

"I really don't think that's an excuse the legal system would smile on."

"Hey, I'm the mayor. Would I do anything illegal?" She smiled at him again, and damned if Nathan's body didn't do a quick lunge. His arm tightened around her waist, tucking her in even closer, and when she moved in the dance, she did things to him he didn't want to think about.

So he didn't. To distract himself, he let his gaze sweep the town, and it didn't escape him that he could see the whole thing in a matter of seconds. The buildings were old, but well cared for. Fresh paint shone in the lights and sidewalks were swept clean. Flower boxes jutted out from window fronts and he presumed that if spring should ever come to the mountains, those boxes would be full of bright flowers.

A couple hundred people crowded the blocked-off streets, and he saw everyone from old couples sitting quietly holding hands to teenaged lovers gazing at each other so intently, he half expected to see tiny cartoon hearts circling their heads.

Keira fit right in here. She was greeted by hugs, kisses, teasing laughter and shouts, and Nathan wondered briefly what it must be like to so thoroughly belong somewhere. He hadn't known that feeling since he was a kid. And he had, over the years, done everything he could to *keep* from belonging anywhere in particular. Yet he could see that Keira thrived on the very kind of life he'd avoided.

Overhead, the moon peeked through a wisp of clouds and shone down onto the town, bathing it in a silvery glow that made it look almost magical. Which was a ridiculous thought, since Hunter's Landing was clearly no more than a tiny town in between a couple of bigger ones.

If Hunter Palmer hadn't chosen this town—no doubt for the pleasure of building a mansion in a town that shared his name—Nathan would never have known of the place's existence. He wasn't a man to go wandering down unbeaten paths.

He preferred big cities. The anonymity of hotel rooms with an ever-changing sea of faces surrounding him. He had no interest in bonding with a town and people he'd never see again once he got off this mountain.

And yet…

Keira held his hand a little tighter as if she could read his thoughts and was subtly trying to hold him here, to this place.

She felt good in his arms, her curvy little body pressed up close to his, and Nathan could admit, at least to himself, that he wanted her. He hadn't had any intention of making a connection of any sort with the people of this town, but she just wouldn't go the hell away. And was it his fault if his body reacted to hers?

This reaction was chemical, pure and simple.

He'd been so long without a woman sharing his bed that he was reacting to the first female to get close.

Not that she was close.

But the thought of her in his bed was enough to set a flash fire racing through his bloodstream.

"Oh," she said, tipping her head back to stare up at him, "now I *really* have to know what you're thinking. Your face just got all stiff and your eyes went slitty."

"Slitty?"

"It's a word," she argued.

"Barely."

"You're changing the subject."

"Apparently not successfully," he said, not surprised at all that she wasn't willing to back down.

"Once you get to know me," she countered, "you'll know that I don't give up all that easily."

"Trust me," Nathan said, "that much I've already learned."

"Wow!" Her face lit up and her eyes sparkled in the overhead lights. "We're really making progress here, aren't we?"

"Progress?"

"You bet. I know that you get all stiff when you don't want to talk about something, and you know that I'm a little stubborn…"

"A little?"

"…we're practically friends already."

"Friends?"

"Nothing wrong with that, is there?" she asked and came to a stop as the song ended and a new one, one with a raw, savage beat, started up. "You have so many friends you can't use another one?"

No, he didn't have friends. Purposely. That need had been satisfied then discarded ten years ago. Now his life was streamlined. Just the way he wanted it.

Nathan let her go gratefully, though he couldn't help but notice just how empty his arms felt without her in them. A warning flag if he'd ever seen one. Keeping a few feet of space between them seemed like the smart move, here. And he'd always been smart enough to protect himself.

"We're not friends, Keira. Friends don't use extortion to get their way."

"Really?" she asked, tipping her head to one side so that her hair fell in a reddish-blond wave to the side of her head, "isn't that what your friend Hunter Palmer did?"

He felt himself stiffen again and couldn't seem to stop it. "Excuse me?"

"Well," she said, linking her arm through his and leading him farther away from the pulsing beat of the song and the jostling crowd on the dance floor, "you clearly don't want to be here, but you're going to stay the month because your old friend asked you to in his will. So, isn't that extortion?"

He supposed it was and hadn't he been thinking pretty much along the same lines earlier today? "You can be extremely annoying."

"I've heard that before."

"Again, not surprising."

"Come on, Nathan," she said, tugging at his arm, "I think it's time I fed you. Maybe your attitude will improve once you've tasted Clearwater's lasagna."

He didn't want to spend more time with her. She had a way of getting into his head that he wasn't entirely comfortable with. So he stopped dead, and Keira jolted back into him.

"Hey, a little warning before a sudden stop might be a good thing."

"Sorry. But I think I've seen enough," he said. "I came to the potluck and now, if you don't mind, I'd like to go back to the house."

"You haven't eaten yet," she said.

"Not hungry."

"Liar."

He shoved his hands into his jacket pockets and gave her a look that had been known to send hotel managers scurrying for cover. "Are you going to take me back or not?"

"You bet. As soon as we eat."

"Damn it, Keira—"

"You have to eat, Nathan. You might as well do it here."

When he didn't budge, she prodded. "You're not scared of us, are you?"

"Us?"

"The town." She spread her arms wide as if encompassing everyone there in a hug. "Hunter's Landing. You a little worried that if you stick around for a while, you just might get to like us?"

"Don't you get it?" he asked, suddenly feeling that, if he wasn't rude, she'd never listen to him. "I'm not here to make friends. I'm here because I have to be. I owe it—" He stopped himself before he gave her more information than he wanted to. "I'm not interested in liking or disliking your town. I just want to put in my time and get back to my life."

"Wow." She blinked up at him. "You did it again."

Nathan sighed and asked the question he knew he shouldn't. "What?"

"Turned on the rude," she said. "It's pretty impressive, really, just how easy it is for you to get all crabby and nasty."

"You don't listen to me otherwise."

"Oh," she said, smiling again like nothing was wrong, "I listen, I just don't pay attention. There's a difference. And whether you want to admit it or not Nathan Barrister, you're hungry. You may not want to be here, but since you *are* here, you might as well eat. Right?"

How was a man supposed to argue with that kind of twisted logic? She grabbed his arm and tugged him toward a long line of tables piled high with what looked like every kind of food imaginable.

Nathan felt like a petulant child and he didn't like it. No point in being stubborn about this, though. There was no way out. He couldn't *walk* back up the mountain. And he wasn't going to ask someone else to drive him up. So he'd wait. He'd eat. And once he got back up the mountain, he'd call his damn pilot and tell him to fire up the engines.

No way was he going to stay for the whole month. A couple of days in Keira Sanders's company was enough to convince him to leave while he still could.

For the next hour, Keira watched him with some amusement.

Nathan probably wouldn't be happy to hear it, but she found it pretty entertaining watching him try to dodge the town's gratitude. Every time someone stepped up to say thank you, Nathan turned into a stone statue. He would nod politely, close down his features and then turn away, only to be met by yet another grateful citizen.

What was it about this man that was so intriguing? She couldn't quite figure it out. But seeing him squirm uncomfortably around her friends and neighbors was just captivating enough that she wanted to know him better. To slip under the walls he'd erected around himself. To get past the arrogant stance and condescending tone to the man who lived within.

Or was she just fooling herself?

Maybe there was no inner Nathan to meet. Maybe he was just who he appeared to be. Rich, aloof, disinterested. But she didn't believe that. She'd seen the quick flash of humor in his eyes before he deliberately stamped it out, and she was willing to put in the time to see if she could reach past his barriers.

Why?

She hadn't figured that out yet.

Oh, sure. She was working double-time to make sure he didn't leave town before his month was up. But this was more personal than insuring a bequest to the town she loved. This was getting to be…interesting.

When her cell phone rang, Keira glanced at the screen, noted the number and got up to walk farther away from Nathan and the crowd to answer it. She threw him a finger-wave as she moved off and smiled to herself at the panic that zipped across his face.

Couldn't really blame him for the panic as Sallye and Margie, the town's two most talkative women, took up position on either side of him. Keira left him to his own devices as she stepped into the doorway of the flower shop and flipped her phone open.

"Hi, Kelly!"

"Hey, big sister, how's it going?" Kelly Sanders sounded like she was down the street instead of calling from her home in London.

Keira didn't even want to think about what kind of charges were going to be adding up on her cell phone. But she was so glad to talk to her younger sister, she wasn't going to worry about it.

"Everything's good," Keira shouted to be heard over the band who, even now, was cranking up the decibels to ear shattering level.

"What's going on?" Kelly demanded, then, after a heartbeat, whined, "It's a block party, isn't it? Everyone's having a good time and I'm not there."

"Yeah, but you're in Europe. Really good times, remember?"

"True," she said wistfully. "Usually I love it here, but I hate knowing life is going on at home without me."

Well, that was typical Kelly. She had always wanted to be in the center of things. Even when she was a little girl, Kelly wasn't satisfied with being in the background. Their mother used to say that Kelly had been born in a hurry and had just never stopped running.

Keira really missed her. They were each other's only family now, and this last year, when Kelly had been living in England, Keira had had a hard time of it.

"I'll tell everyone you said hi," she said and glanced down the street, making sure Nathan hadn't bolted for freedom. Nope, he was still there, sandwiched between the two very nice, very chatty older ladies. Keira grinned, leaned against the shingled wall of the flower shop and said, "So what's going on?"

"Oh, Tony's taking me to Paris for the weekend and I wanted to let you know I wouldn't be home for our Saturday night phone call."

Tony—also known as Stewart Anthony Brookhurst, was CEO of some huge conglomerate based in England and, for the last six months, the main topic of all of Kelly's conversations.

"Paris, very nice," Keira said and tried to keep the sigh of envy from slipping from her soul.

She'd had plenty of plans of her own years ago. She'd wanted to finish college, travel, see the world. But in the blink of an eye, her plans—her world—had changed. Not that she regretted being there for Kelly, for putting her own life plans on hold to see to it that her little sister went to college. She didn't resent the fact that while she had stayed here, in the town she loved, Kelly had gone off on the adventures that Keira had once dreamed of.

And, if she did feel occasional spikes of envy jabbing at her, she'd managed so far to hide them from the sister she loved.

"I know," Kelly said with a laugh. "Who would have thought that I'd be saying stuff like that? *Paris for the weekend.* But you know, K, I really love it here. I mean, I miss home and everybody, you especially, but I love living in London. I even like the rain!"

"I know." She heard that love in Kelly's voice every time they spoke. This was supposed to have been a one-year stint—a year that was almost over—in London, for the international bank that had hired Kelly right out of college. But Keira had been preparing herself for months now, to be ready for the day when Kelly announced that she would be *staying* in Europe.

Kelly loved everything about England and now that she was seriously dating a man who had been born and raised there, the chances of her ever moving back to Hunter's Landing were slimmer than ever.

"So what's going on at home, besides the party I'm not at," she asked.

Keira shook off the gloomy thoughts that had settled over her like some sort of shroud and forced a smile into her voice. "We've got our first guest in the lake lodge."

"Oh my God! You're kidding! What's he like? Did you see the inside of the place? Is it fabulous?"

Keira laughed. God, she missed her little sister. "Not kidding, he seems nice, saw the house, it's amazing."

"C'mon," Kelly whined. "There's gotta be more than that. You've been telling me about that house for a year now. So what's it like?"

"It's so gorgeous, you wouldn't believe it. Awesome views of the lake—built of glass and wood and stone, and there's a fireplace big enough to stand up in."

"Oh, wow."

"I'll say."

"And the guy?"

"What about him?"

"*'He seems nice?'*" Kelly laughed. "Please. Give me more than that."

More? What could she say? That he was arrogant and irritating and altogether too attractive? That she was spending too much time thinking about *him* when she should have been worrying about keeping him in the lodge long enough to fulfill the requirements of the will?

"What's his name, at least," Kelly demanded.

"Nathan." There. That was safe information. "Nathan Barrister."

"*Whoa.* Barrister? Like in the Barrister Hotel Barristers?"

"I don't know," Keira said with a shrug her sister couldn't see. "I…maybe."

"Nathan Barrister was in London a couple of months ago. Had a meeting at my bank. Tell me what yours looks like and I'll tell you if it's him."

"Tall. Dark. Pale blue eyes."

"Snotty twist to his mouth?" Kelly asked.

"Not exactly snotty," Keira argued.

"Woo hoo," Kelly crowed. "It *is* him. And you *like* him."

"Dial it down, Kel," Keira said, knowing it was way too late to put the lid back down on that particular box. Kelly was already enjoying herself.

"I don't believe this. Nathan Barrister in Hunter's Landing? That's too funny."

"Why's it funny?" She stiffened at the amusement in her sister's voice and felt like she should be defending the man for some reason.

"Well, he's just such a *stick.* The man has no sense of humor and one look out of those eyes and you practically freeze over. And I saw my boss's face after his meeting with Barrister. You remember I told you that my boss is mean enough to give the boogeyman nightmares?"

"Yeah…"

"When Barrister left his office, my boss was *pale* and shaking."

"Oh."

"Seriously, K," Kelly said, her voice dropping. It was

a strain to hear her over the crash of the band and the swell of laughter and conversation rising up over Main Street. "If you're thinking about falling for this guy, don't do it."

"Oh, please." Keira sighed, shook her hair back from her face and said, "He's here as part of that will I told you about. If he stays for the month, if the rest of them each stay for a month, the town is going to get a heck of a lot of money that we really need. And that's all there is to it. I just said he was attractive, I didn't say I was going after him."

"You didn't say he was attractive!" Kelly's voice shrieked so high that Keira jerked the phone away from her ear.

"I didn't?"

"No. K, don't do this. Don't let yourself care about this guy. Remember what happened with—"

"Don't go there, okay?" Keira interrupted her quickly, not willing to take a forced march down memory lane. "And let's remember here just which one of us is the *older* sister."

"I know," Kelly said, "it's just that you're so—"

"So *what* exactly?"

"I don't know. Never mind. Just be careful, okay?"

"I'm always careful, Kelly. Trust me. Nothing's going to happen." Even if she wanted something to happen, Nathan had already made it perfectly clear that *he* didn't, so what could happen?

Keira peeked around the edge of the flower shop wall to stare down the street at Nathan again—big mistake. He was watching for her. Even from a distance, his gaze slammed into hers with a punch that was nearly physical. Keira sucked in a gulp of air and reached out blindly with her right hand to slap it against the wall in an effort to balance herself. It didn't help much.

A flicker of heat kicked into life in the pit of her stomach and rolled through her like a storm-pitched wave crashing onto shore. She felt her world rock and had to fight to right it again.

"K?" Kelly's voice was in her ear. "Are you okay?"

"Yeah," she lied, swallowing hard past the knot of need that was lodged firmly in her throat. She couldn't look away from Nathan's eyes. "I'm fine. Don't worry about anything."

"But—"

"Look. Send me a postcard from Paris, okay?"

"Sure, but—"

"Bye, honey, be safe." Keira flipped the phone closed and straightened up just as Nathan headed toward her.

Five

Nathan had had enough.

His ears were ringing and the good manners his grandmother had drummed into him were strained now to the snapping point. He'd excused himself from the two older women who had seemed determined to trap him on Main Street forever, and now he was going to get Keira to take him back to the lodge.

He should have driven himself.

Then he wouldn't be waiting around for anyone. He wasn't a man who liked being dependent on someone else for anything. His insides tightened as people milled past him, laughing, talking, dancing. He wasn't a part of them and never would be. Didn't *want* to be. And the more time he spent with all of them, the more clear that feeling became.

He didn't know why the hell he hadn't left the mountains already. He didn't *have* to honor a promise made in college to a man long-dead. Hell, he could donate the twenty million himself and get out of this mess now.

And with that thought firmly in his mind, his steps quickened toward Keira. Her gaze locked with his and he told himself to pay no attention to the brilliant green of her eyes or the worried twist of her mouth. He refused to notice how the light dazzled the ends of her reddish-blond hair, making it almost glow in a soft halo around her head. And damned if he would remember just how good she felt when her body was pressed against his during their dance.

As he came closer, she shoved her cell phone into the front pocket of her jeans and inhaled deeply enough that her breasts rose and then fell with the rush of her sigh.

If his body tightened suddenly, desperately, he ignored it.

"Hi," she said and, somehow, her voice carried over the other sounds on the street. "Enjoying yourself?"

He frowned at her. "Yeah, it's been great. I've eaten, I've danced and I've listened to enough thank-yous to last me a lifetime, so if you don't mind, I'd like a ride back to the lodge."

"Sure."

"That easy?" He felt one eyebrow quirk. He hadn't expected her to give in without trying to talk him into staying longer.

"Why not?" she asked and looked away from him, shifting her gaze to sweep across the town square. She sighed again and this time her voice was so soft, he almost missed it. "I just wanted you to see Hunter's

Landing. To meet some of the people, so you'd know who you and your friends are helping."

"Thank you." He heard the sarcasm in his own voice but didn't bother to try to take the sting out of it.

"I can take you by the clinic for a quick look on the way back. Then you can see exactly what we're planning."

"Not necessary."

Nathan blew out a frustrated breath. Everything in him was clamoring to be gone from this place. To pick up the threads of his life and get back to living the way he knew best. He didn't do well with other people. Didn't care to. And yet now…

Screw it.

"How about that ride?"

Frowning, she said, "You're just determined not to enjoy yourself, aren't you?"

"Was that a requirement?"

She muttered, "Kelly was right. You really are scary, aren't you?"

"What?"

"Nothing." Reluctantly, she shrugged and said, "Let's go."

He followed her to her truck and when she stumbled over a crack in the road, Nathan lunged forward to grab her before she could fall. Spinning her around, he pulled her in close and she laughed up at him. The woman was so changeable, he could hardly keep up.

"Thanks, didn't see that."

"Weren't looking, you mean."

Her hands were on his upper arms and even through the thick leather of his coat, he felt the heat in her touch and wanted more. Wanted to feel her hands on his bare skin, run his own hands over every curve of her body. Hear her sigh as he buried himself inside her.

The images in his mind were suddenly so clear, so overpowering, he could hardly draw a breath past the hot fist tightening around his lungs.

He willed himself to speak. "It's a wonder you're not covered in bruises the way you stumble around."

"What makes you think I'm not?" she asked, still smiling.

He pulled in another deep breath of cold, mountain air and hoped it would help chill the fire in his blood. "What the hell are you doing to me?" he demanded.

"Depends, Nathan," she said, her smile fading as her brilliant green eyes darkened with a need he recognized. "What do you *want* me to do to you?"

"I'm not interested in a short affair," he said tightly, despite the fact that his body clamored for just that.

"Well, who asked you?" She pulled free of his grasp, straightened up and shook her hair back from her face. "Jeez, save a girl from a fall and then accuse *her* of trying to seduce *you*. Nice. Very nice."

He pushed one hand through his hair and wondered why in the hell he tried talking to her anyway. "Can we just get in the damn truck?"

She dug her keys out of her pocket and bounced them on her palm. "You know, you were the one looking at me like you wanted to gobble me up."

He blew out another breath and glared at her. "Call it temporary insanity."

"Wow, one compliment after another," she said and turned for the truck. "You're really on a roll here, Barrister."

He stood just where he was and watched her open the driver's side door and step up into the cab. "You're an infuriating woman, did you know that?"

She glanced back at him over her shoulder. "Believe it or not, that's been said before."

"My sympathies to the poor bastard, whoever he was."

Her face froze up and her eyes shuttered as effectively as if she'd slapped on a pair of dark glasses. "He doesn't need your sympathy, Nathan. And neither do I. So, you getting in the truck or are you going to walk back up the mountain?"

Over the next week or so, every time Keira drove up the mountain, she was half afraid she'd find Nathan gone. After a *really* quiet ride back from the block party, she had dropped him off at the lodge and had hardly waited for his feet to hit the dirt before she gunned the engine and went home. It still embarrassed her to think about driving off in a huff like that.

She never should have let him get to her—couldn't understand why she had. But that little dig about giving his sympathies to whichever man had last been in her life had come a little too quickly after Kelly had brought up the same damn thing.

It wasn't that Keira was sensitive about her past; she just didn't like being reminded of what an idiot she'd been once upon a time.

But that was the past and this was now. And all that mattered *now* was making sure Nathan didn't leave before his month was up. She was pretty sure he was tired of having her show up on his doorstep every day, but she kept visiting him anyway, because she could practically *see* his need to leave vibrating in the air all around him.

And she wouldn't let that happen.

Parking the truck in the drive, she hopped out, slammed the door and headed for the front door. Dark clouds hung heavy over the mountains and the air felt thick with the promise of more snow. As much as she loved winter in the mountains, she was really ready for spring. Unfortunately, it looked as if nature didn't feel the same way.

She shivered, dug her hands into her jacket pockets and quickened her step, only to stop when she heard Nathan's voice shout, "Back here."

Surprised to find him outside and away from the laptop that he clung to like his last link with civilization, Keira headed down the drive. She saw him at the lake's edge and she wasn't ashamed to admit, at least to herself, that the man was really sigh-worthy.

He wore that dark green cashmere sweater again over jeans that looked worn and comfortable. His brown leather jacket gave him a piratical air, and the wind tossed his hair across his forehead, making him look more free than she could remember seeing him before. Her heart jumped a little and her mouth went dry.

She could be in some serious trouble here. Especially if he started looking at her the way he had the night of the party.

"What're you doing?" she called as her boots crunched on the gravel drive.

He gave her a quick look, then shifted his gaze back to the steel gray surface of the lake. "Just looking. Needed some air."

"Really?" she teased as she walked up to stop beside him. "I thought you were very happy breathing canned air and looking at nature through the beauty of clean glass windows."

He snorted. "Let's just say I'm feeling a little cabin fever."

There it was again. She could see how ready he was to chuck the whole month and escape from what he no doubt considered captivity. So what she had to do was take his mind off it.

"I can cure that."

"How?"

"Take a walk with me." She threaded her arm through the crook of his and smiled up at him.

"It's freezing out here," he reminded her.

"If we keep moving, we won't feel it." She tugged at his arm. "Come on. When's the last time you took a walk along a lake as beautiful as this one?"

His gaze swept out over the wide expanse of water and the pine-tree-studded shoreline before turning back to her. "Never."

"Way too long," she assured him and started walking. His long legs outdistanced hers, and Keira caught herself half running to keep up before she pulled back on his arm and said, "It's not a race, you know. You don't actually get a prize for reaching the other side."

He stopped, smirked a little, then shrugged. "Point taken. But I'm not used to just strolling."

"It's okay," Keira said, enjoying the flash of warmth in his too-cool blue eyes. "You can learn."

They walked in companionable silence for a few

minutes before she said, "The bears will be waking up soon."

"Bears?"

"Oh, yeah. Black ones and brown ones. Mamas and babies. They'll be trolling through backyards and tipping over trash cans looking for food or trouble."

"Bears." He shook his head. "Can't imagine living somewhere I could expect to bump into a bear."

"Funny, huh?" she asked, tipping her face up to the darkening clouds, "I can't imagine living anywhere else."

"You were raised here?"

"Yep. Born in Lake Tahoe, raised here. We didn't have a clinic back then. Now our new moms don't have to take that trek over the mountain for medical help." She grinned and patted his arm with her free hand. "And thanks to you, our clinic's going to be even better than it already is."

"You've thanked me enough."

"Not really," she said, "but I'll let it go."

"Thank you."

"For now."

He snorted.

"What about you?" she asked in the silence, "Where are you from?"

"Everywhere," he said, turning his gaze on the wind-whipped water of the lake again.

"That's not an answer, just so you know."

"I was born in Massachusetts. Grew up on the east coast."

Amazing how the man could give information and still make it seem like so little. But Keira wasn't a woman to be dissuaded easily. She dug a little deeper.

"Your family still there?"

"No family," he said shortly, and his gorgeous blue eyes squinted into the wind racing past them.

"I'm sorry."

"No reason to be. You couldn't know."

"Well, I am, anyway," she said and squeezed his arm companionably. "My folks died when I was in college," she said, thinking that maybe if she gave a little, he'd be willing to give a little, too. "They went skiing. Got caught in an avalanche."

His gaze shifted to hers. "Now I'm sorry."

She looked up at him and smiled. "Thank you. It was really hard. I still miss them so much."

"I was ten," he said. "Car accident."

A few words, but said so tightly, Keira could feel the old pain still welling inside him. At least she'd been grown when she lost her parents. She couldn't even imagine how lonely and terrifying it would have been to be a child and lose the safety of your own little world.

"God, Nathan, that's terrible."

"A long time ago," he reminded her. "Had my grandmother. Dad's mom. She took me in."

"That couldn't have been easy for her," Keira said, then stumbled on a piece of wood jutting up into the rocky trail.

Nathan caught her by tightening his grip on her arm and keeping her steady. "It wasn't much of a hardship. She sent me to boarding school, and I was only home for a month every summer."

"She *what?*"

He blinked at her, clearly surprised by her reaction. What kind of people farmed out ten-year-old kids to boarding schools? What kind of grandparent couldn't see that the child left in her care was in pain and needed more than the impersonal attention of someone *paid* to watch over him?

"It was a very good school," he said.

"Oh, I'm sure." A spurt of anger shot through Keira on behalf of a child who no longer existed. "No brothers or sisters?"

"Nope. You?"

God, he had been all alone with a grandmother too busy to give him what he must have craved. A sense of belonging. A sense of safety. Keira couldn't even imagine what that must have been like for him, and a part of her warmed up to his frosty nature a little more. After all, if he'd been so cut off as a child, how could she possibly expect the man to be open to possibilities?

He was watching her, waiting for her to answer his question, and so she gave him a smile that didn't let him in on the fact that she was really feeling sorry for the boy he'd once been.

"I have a sister. Kelly. She's younger than me and was still in high school when our folks were killed. So, I came home from school, watched over her and started running the family diner."

He frowned. "The coffee shop in town?"

"You noticed it? Yep. The Lakeside was my dad's baby. It's small, but it's been good to us. Made it possible for me to get Kelly into college—well, the diner and a few good loans."

"What about you?" he asked. "You didn't go back to school?"

"No," she said, still irritated with his grandmother for some bizarre reason. "I meant to, I really did. But then

Kelly was in college, and no way could we afford for both of us to go. And when she graduated, I'd already hired a manager for the diner and was running for mayor, so…" She shrugged.

"Your sister should have taken her turn in town to give you a chance to go to school."

Keira shook her head. "No, she got a tremendous job offer right out of school and there was no way she could not take it."

He was silent, but the quiet held a lot of disapproval.

"You could go back to college now," he pointed out.

"Oh, yeah," Keira said, laughing shortly. "Just what I want to do. Go to school with a bunch of kids. Sounds like a great time."

"What's your sister doing now?"

"She's living in London," Keira said, defensive of a little sister who didn't need defending. "She loves England," she added with a wistful sigh. "She sends me pictures that make me want to pack my bags and go there for myself."

"Why don't you?"

"I can't just leave because I *want* to. I have responsibilities to this town."

He sighed, frowned and turned slitted eyes on her. "Is that a not so subtle hint?"

"I wasn't going for subtle," she admitted, smiling up at him despite the glower in his eyes. "Just for a reminder about the responsibilities *you* and the others have to Hunter's Landing."

"I'd never heard of your town until a month ago," he reminded her, "and a month from now, I will have forgotten it."

"Well, don't we feel special," she mused.

"It's nothing personal," he said. "It's just…"

"None of that really matters, does it? You agreed to the terms of the will and—" The toe of her boot caught under a root and she would have gone sprawling if Nathan hadn't steadied her again.

"You're dangerous," he snapped. "Why don't you pay more attention to where you're walking?"

"Hey, I have you here to catch me."

"Don't count on that."

"I am, though," Keira said, blocking his way by stepping in front of him before she stopped dead. "We're all counting on you. You and your friends."

The wind sliced in off the lake and cut at them like a knife straight out of a freezer. Keira's hair swept across her eyes and she plucked it free so she could look at Nathan.

He didn't look happy, but what was new about that? His gaze was locked with hers and his mouth was tightened into a grim slash that told her exactly what he was thinking.

"I know you don't want to hear it," Keira said and reached out to put both hands on his forearms. And even through the icy brown leather jacket, she felt the strength of him, tightly leashed. "But it's true. I can't even tell you how important it is to all of us that you stay for the month."

"Keira—"

"I know, I know," she said, lifting both hands in a mock surrender. "You don't want to hear about this anymore."

"The night of the town party," he admitted quietly, "I had every intention of calling my pilot and flying out of here."

"But you didn't," she said lightly, despite the quick tightening around her insides.

"That doesn't mean I won't," he pointed out. "I don't want you—or anyone—counting on me. For anything."

"That's a hard way to live," she said.

"It's my way."

"It doesn't have to be," Keira said, her voice a whisper that was nearly lost in the swirl of the wind. Why was she doing this? Why did she care how Nathan Barrister lived his life?

He laughed shortly, and the sound was so surprising that Keira blinked at him.

"I *like* my life just the way it is," he said. "I'm not interested in changing it."

"Just like you're not interested in a one-month affair."

His jaw clenched.

Oops.

She didn't know why she'd said that. But now that it was back out in the open between them, she wasn't sure how to *un*-say it, either.

"Keira…"

A puff of white danced on the wind and flew between them as if trying to end their conversation.

"Was that…?" he asked.

"Snow," she said.

And in that split second, several more flakes of snow whipped around them, carried on the wind that snapped and rattled at the pine trees. The temperature dropped what felt like twenty degrees and the lowering clouds looked black and threatening.

"Of course it's snow. For God's sake, does spring *ever* get here?" He inhaled sharply, deeply, and looked at her as if there was something more he wanted to say.

The look in his eyes was nearly electric. Despite the

snowflakes just beginning to flurry around them, she felt heat arcing between them.

Her heartbeat was jittering in her chest, her blood was pumping hot and thick in her veins, and she had the most overpowering urge to reach up and smooth his hair back from his forehead.

Instead, she curled her fingers into her palms and took a deep breath. "It's coming down harder. We should start back."

Six

By the time they reached the lodge, snow had dusted their hair and shoulders and was thick enough in the air that every breath tasted like ice.

When Keira would have turned down the driveway to head for her truck, Nathan caught her elbow and tugged her up the back steps to the house by the lake.

"Nathan…"

He stopped on the top step, looked down into her soft green eyes and said, "You might as well wait out the storm here."

She hunched deeper into her jacket, swung her snow-dusted hair out of her eyes and said, "It might not stop for a few hours."

Glad to hear it, he almost said and was glad he'd managed to clamp his jaw shut. But the truth was, he didn't want to go back into that too-damned-quiet lodge. It was bad enough to be trapped there in the silence when the sun was shining. He had a feeling that being alone with the falling snow and lowering clouds would make him feel as though he were buried alive in a dark cave. Not something he really wanted to experience.

"And it might stop in a few minutes," he pointed out, but, as if to prove that prediction false, the wind kicked up and the snow flew in frenzied flurries.

"If I was home right now," Keira said, "I'd make myself some hot chocolate."

"I can probably handle that," he said. "Or, there's some excellent brandy."

She climbed up a step, coming that much closer to him, and the depths in her green eyes called to him, reached for him. "Brandy would be good, too. Got anything to eat?"

He held out one hand and waited for her to take it. When she did, his fingers folded tightly around hers. "There's plenty of stuff in the fridge."

She took the last step that brought her beside him and gave him a smile that warmed him through, despite the icy wind and the snow sneaking beneath the collar of his jacket. "Then why are we still standing in the storm?"

They walked across the covered deck, stepped into the mudroom and pulled off their jackets and boots. Then, together, they went into the kitchen. The room was cavernous, with built in niches for the stainless steel appliances and a mile of granite counter. The walls were painted to give them an antiqued finish, and the colors were warm cream and brown, making the kitchen seem cozy even in the midst of a storm.

"Let's get that brandy first, worry about food later," Nathan said, and led the way from the kitchen to the great room.

"Good plan," she said and shivered a little as she followed him down the hall.

A fire was blazing in the hearth and Keira moved straight toward it as Nathan walked to the wet bar. He poured them each a drink, then walked to join her by the fire. Handing her one of the crystal snifters, he watched the amber liquid swirl in the bottom of his glass for a long moment before he took a sip.

He swallowed and felt the alcohol fueled fire rush through him as he shifted his gaze to Keira. Firelight played on her skin and danced in her eyes. The ends of her hair shone with a nearly incandescent light and when she lifted her glass to her lips, everything inside him tightened.

After taking a sip, she blew out a breath, smiled and looked up at him. "Wow. Well, that warms you up fast, doesn't it?"

Nathan ground his teeth together and then took a sip of his own brandy. The heat it produced was nothing like the *other* kind of heat swamping him. Just looking at Keira made him burn.

For more than a week now, he had tried not to think about her, to put this insane attraction out of his mind. But he hadn't been able to manage it. When he closed his eyes, he saw her. When he dreamed, he touched her. When he thought he would go out of his mind from the silence in this place, she arrived and he nearly went out of his mind for different reasons entirely.

She sat down on the stone hearth, the fire at her back,

and looked up at him as she cradled the brandy snifter between her palms. "So, Nathan, are you the Barrister Hotel guy?"

One eyebrow rose and he took another sip of his brandy, welcoming the steady fire. "Hotel guy? Yeah. I suppose I am. How'd you know?"

She smiled. "Just a guess. Hunter's Landing isn't exactly on the moon. We get newspapers and magazines here, too. Which one of your hotels is your favorite?"

He shrugged carelessly. "I don't really have a favorite, they're all top-of-the-line establishments, each of them with their own unique pluses and minuses."

"Boy, feel the enthusiasm."

"I'm sorry?"

"Well, come on, Nathan, you own four-star hotels—"

"Five-star," he amended automatically.

"Right. In beautiful, exotic places all over the world. You talk about them as if they're nothing special. As if they're no different from any other exclusive hotels. Is that really what you think?"

Nathan frowned, sat down beside her and instantly appreciated the heat of the fire warming his back. "It's the family business, Keira. They're valuable properties with impeccable reputations that I work hard to maintain."

"Uh-huh," she said and nudged his upper arm with her shoulder. "And do you ever drop in on one in say…Paris, or Dublin…just for fun?"

"No," he said and wondered why he cared that she looked disappointed at his statement. "I have a rigorous schedule I adhere to. The managers of the hotels know when I'm coming, know to have everything ready for my inspection and—"

She sighed.

"What?"

"Do they salute? Click their heels together when you walk into a room?"

He scowled at her. "I'm not a general or something."

"Could have fooled me," she muttered, and took another sip of brandy. "Seriously, do you scare all the people who work for you? I bet you do."

"Certainly not," Nathan said and wondered why he suddenly sounded so damn pompous, even to himself.

"You know," she said, lifting her brandy glass to peer at the room through the amber liquid, "if you changed up your *schedule* once in a while, you might actually catch people unaware. Find out what life in your hotels is really like."

He stared at her, but she wasn't looking at him. Her words, though, were running through his brain as if they'd been etched in neon. Funny, but he'd never thought to do something like that. He was a man who lived his life as efficiently as possible. And to do that, he required a schedule. But...

"You mean, I should show up when they're not expecting me?"

"Why not?" she mused. "They're *your* hotels, aren't they?"

"Yes, but a schedule is necessary to maintain some kind of order."

"And if the kids know that daddy's coming home, they're on their best behavior."

Frowning, Nathan kept staring at her until she finally turned and looked at him, her eyes wide.

"What?" she asked.

"I can't believe I never thought of that."

"Me, neither," she said, smiling. "For heaven's sake, Nathan, do you *ever* do something that you don't have scheduled? Do you ever take a little time out for yourself? You're wound so tight, it gives *me* a headache."

He sighed and shrugged. "In my world, there's no time for relaxing."

"You should make time." She turned on the hearth, laid one hand on his forearm and asked, "For instance, when you're at one of your fabulous, oh-so-exclusive hotels, do you ever take a swim? Get a massage? Sightsee?"

"No. I'm not there for pleasure—"

"Why not?"

"Because…"

"People all over the world want to go to your hotels to experience something amazing. I've seen some of them on TV. And in magazines. God, the one in London, I would actually kill to stay in."

He smiled, picturing the stately stone entrance of the London Barrister with its sweeping marble floors and Old World chandeliers in the lobby.

"It is beautiful," he mused, surprised that he hadn't really appreciated the place until seeing it through Keira's enthusiasm.

"It's amazing," she said with a sigh. "Some rock star held an interview in the penthouse suite and the news covered it—there was an incredible view of London."

"The view from the owner's suite is even more impressive," he told her, picturing it vividly now in his mind. "You can see Big Ben in the distance and the Millennium Wheel."

"The huge Ferris wheel!" she cried and grabbed his

arm hard. "Have you ridden it?" She paused, and said, "Of course you haven't. Honestly, Nathan, don't you ever have any *fun?*"

A little insulted, he said, "Sure I do."

"Prove it. Name one thing you've done just for fun in the last month," she challenged.

"I sat on a stone hearth letting a beautiful woman insult me."

She tipped her head to one side, gave him a smile that made his heart jitter in his chest and repeated, *"Beautiful?"*

"Figures that's the part you heard."

Her smile brightened into a grin. "Well, *duh.*"

He really enjoyed the flash of humor in her eyes. And for the first time in way too long, he realized there wasn't a steel band wrapped around his middle. There was no pressure pounding through him. No hurry to get work done. To check his e-mail. To leave the lodge.

Because suddenly and completely, there was simply nowhere else on earth he'd rather be.

The quiet between them stretched on for another minute or two, the only sound in the room, the snap and hiss of the fire behind them. Shadows stretched across the room and, outside, dots of white swirled in ever changing patterns driven by the wind.

"I envy you," she said quietly. "All the places you've seen."

"You like traveling?"

"Never really traveled much, but yeah, I think I would." She folded her legs up beneath her on the stone, her white socks standing out brilliantly against her dark denim jeans. "I had big plans," she admitted. "When I was a teenager, I went to bookstores and bought street maps of foreign cities. If you had dropped me into the middle of Paris, I could have found my way around blindfolded, I studied those maps so often. London, Dublin, Barcelona, Rome, oh…*Venice*." Her voice took on a dreamy quality that tugged at something deep inside him. "I wanted to drink wine while riding in a gondola. And see the windmills in Holland, and the Swiss Alps…"

"But…"

"But," she said, giving him a dazzling smile and lifting her glass for another sip of brandy, "life happened. I had to take care of Kelly, and then I got busy with the town and…"

"You stopped reading your maps?"

"Oh, no," she said, "I've still got them all and I still pore over them and plan trips and, one of these days, I'll get away." She looked down into her glass and asked, "What about you? When the month is up, where do you go next?"

"Barbados for a couple of weeks, then Madrid."

She sighed. "It sounds wonderful."

"Barbados or Madrid?"

"Both. But Barbados first. A tropical island." She sighed again.

"A beautiful one," he agreed.

She leaned her head against his shoulder and said, "Show me."

"Can't. Don't have any pictures of it."

"No," she said softly, "Draw me a picture with words. Show it to me through your memories of the place."

Nathan frowned down at the top of her head and tried to give her what she wanted. He thought about the

Barbados Barrister for a long moment, bringing it up in his mind, then slowly said, "It's our newest hotel. Only been open a few months. It sits right on the beach, stretches out almost a block. It has five stories for guest rooms and the sixth floor is the owner's suite." His voice warmed as his memories thickened and the ease of sharing them became more comfortable. "The views stretch on forever. The ocean is so blue you're not sure if you're looking at the sea or the sky."

"Keep going," she said.

He smiled. "There are palm trees and sand so white it hurts to look at it. Green-and-white striped umbrellas surround an infinity pool, and waiters dressed in green shirts and white pants carry trays of drinks to the people lounging poolside."

"More," she said, nestling in closer.

The feel of her leaning into him, the heat of the fire behind them and the quiet of the house all made for a feeling of intimacy that Nathan hadn't allowed himself to feel in years.

"Inside the hotel," he continued, "the wood is pale, almost gold. The windows are always open, and the sea wind sweeps through the lobby where pots of flowers and trailing vines make it seem almost like a jungle." He rested his head on top of hers. "There are deck chairs on a wide, white porch that stretches the length of the first floor, and people sit out there, sometimes all day, just to watch the ocean. And the restaurant has an outside deck where you can dine and watch the sunset."

"Sounds wonderful."

"Actually," he said, not a little surprised himself, "it really is."

She raised her head and smiled up at him. "I'm going to buy a map of Barbados," she said, "and I'm putting that hotel on my list."

He smoothed her hair back from her face, his fingertips lingering on the softness of her skin. She closed her eyes at his touch and shivered a little as his fingers slid down to her jaw.

"I'll put your name on the VIP list," he whispered, threading his fingers through her silky hair again just to enjoy the sensation.

"Nathan?"

"Keira…"

"The storm's still blowing," she said softly, her gaze locked with his. "What will we do while we wait it out?"

"We could eat," he offered.

"True," she said. "Or you could tell me about another of your hotels."

"Or play chess."

"Watch a movie."

"Read."

She nodded and reached up to catch his hand with hers and hold it against her cheek. "All good ideas. But, I have a better idea."

Nathan bit back a groan as she leaned in close to him. His body was hard and tight and every breath now was a victory. If he didn't have her in the next few minutes, he was going to explode. "Yeah?" he asked. "What's that?"

"I think you know," she said and took one more sip of brandy before setting her glass down on the hearth.

Nathan tipped his head back and tossed the last of his brandy down his throat before setting his glass down beside hers.

"Possibly," he said, though a voice in his brain was telling him to stop now before it was too late. But damn it, he wanted her. Keira's image had been haunting him for days—she'd gotten to him more than any other woman he'd ever known. He wasn't used to waiting for something he wanted. Usually, he simply *took* what most women were more than willing to offer. Keira was different. "Why don't you tell me, and I'll let you know if we're on the same page."

"Why don't I show you?" she whispered, and then pressed her mouth to his.

Air.

He probably needed air, because the edges of his vision were blurring and his brain felt as if it had been short-circuited. But breathing didn't seem as important as kissing her—harder, deeper—did.

Nathan groaned, pulled her in tightly to him and opened her mouth with a sweep of his tongue. She sighed into him as he tasted her, tangling their tongues together in a wild, frantic dance of need and promise.

He felt her hands tighten on his shoulders, her fingers digging into the soft fabric of his sweater to brand his skin with match-head dots of flame. Electricity hummed between them and Nathan surrendered to the sensations coursing through him.

He needed her.

Now.

He pulled her into his arms and settled her on his lap. His hands swept up and down her back, defining her curves through the soft knit of her sweater. She sighed heavily, pressed herself more firmly to him and rubbed her body against his.

Nathan's mouth moved over hers like a dying man seeking the only sustenance left in the world. He shared his breath with her and she gave it back to him. Their tongues and lips melded, savored, enjoyed. Nathan slipped both hands beneath the hem of her sweater and his palms slid across her back, his fingertips smoothing over her satiny skin.

She tore her mouth free, let her head fall back and sighed at his touch. "Nathan…"

He lowered his head, kissing her jaw, her neck, following the line of her throat with his lips and teeth and tongue. She shivered in his grasp and fed the need pulsing inside him.

Lifting his head, Nathan looked down at her as his hands, sliding beneath her sweater, swept around her body to find the front clasp on her bra. Deftly, he undid the tiny plastic clip, then pushed her bra free and cupped her breasts in his palms. His thumbs caressed her hardened nipples as his fingers kneaded her soft flesh.

Her hands clutched at his shoulders as he held her tightly to his lap, letting her feel the hard length of him.

Need roared and crashed through Nathan until he could hardly draw breath. He couldn't remember *ever* wanting like this before. He couldn't remember another woman in his life who had pushed him to the razor's edge of rationality. All he could think of was Keira.

All he wanted was Keira.

He didn't care what it might mean.

What it might cost him.

Didn't want to examine every feeling, every ache.

He only wanted to lose himself in her. For this one moment in time, he wanted nothing more than the feel of her beneath his hands and the sensation of burying his body within the hot, tight channel of hers.

"I've got to have you," he whispered, hearing the raw throb in his own voice.

"Me, too," she said, opening her eyes and pulling herself upright, leaning into him. "Oh, Nathan, me, too. Now, okay?"

"Right now." He pulled his hands free of her body, not even thinking about how empty he felt without the warmth of her pouring into him. Then he stood up, set her on her feet and led her across the great room toward the foyer and the majestic staircase that led to the second floor and the master bedroom. With their boots off, their sock feet made almost no noise at all in their rush for the stairs.

She stumbled behind him, kicked an end table and letting go of his hand, hopped ungainly for a minute, whimpering. "Ow, ow…"

Nathan turned, swept her up into his arms and said thickly, "Okay, I'm carrying you from here. I'm not taking any chances with a tumble down the stairs."

"Right, right," she said and leaned in to nibble at his throat as his long legs took the steep stairs two at a time.

He hissed in a breath, took a sharp turn at the head of the stairs and headed for the only bedroom in the place that had been furnished.

Keira looked around quickly as Nathan carried her into the master bedroom. The log walls were pale and the honey-colored floorboards gleamed from a thick coat of polish. A stone hearth, much like the one in the great room, boasted a fire that warmed the room and made it feel, for all its size, cozy. A bank of windows overlooked the lake and the forest and showcased the snow falling steadily.

But Keira didn't really care about the storm or the decor. All she was interested in now was the feel of Nathan's arms around her as he walked toward the huge, dark sleigh bed tucked against the far wall. Her heartbeat thundered in her chest as Nathan set her on her feet, grabbed a corner of the old-fashioned quilt and tossed it to the foot of the bed.

Then he grabbed her again and Keira stopped thinking in favor of *feeling.*

His mouth claimed hers again and her brain sizzled. Every nerve ending she possessed hummed with an awareness she'd never experienced before. His lips and tongue tasted her, tormented her, and she gave as good as she got.

Holding on to his shoulders, she pushed her body against his and rubbed her aching nipples across his chest. She needed him. And that thought was enough to make her splintered brain try to work for a second or two. She knew she should stop. Think about what she was doing.

But a heartbeat later, when Nathan pulled her sweater up and over her head, and bent to take one hardened nipple into his mouth, Keira silently told the cautionary voice in her mind to shut up.

Seven

Keira groaned gently as his mouth closed over first one nipple, then the next. His lips, tongue and teeth teased her already aching flesh until her whole body felt as though it were on full alert. She felt his touch in every cell. Her blood pumped thick and hot through her veins and when she closed her eyes and tipped her head back, she could have sworn she actually saw fireworks bursting in electric flashes of heat and color.

She held his head to her, half afraid that he might stop what he was doing. Her fingers speared through his thick, soft, black hair and when he sighed against her flesh, she felt the heat of his breath brush her skin in an ereal caress.

He dropped his hands to the waistband of her jeans nd, in just moments, he had the button and zipper undone and was sliding them, along with her pale ivory panties, down the length of her legs. She helped as much as she could, stepping out of her jeans and lifting first one foot, then the other, so he could pull her socks off.

The air in the room felt cool against her skin, despite the fire in the hearth. She listened to the snap and hiss of the flames on logs and let the sound fill her mind until all that remained was the music of the fire and Nathan's breath against her body.

She smiled up at him and tugged at the hem of his sweater, fingers curling into the soft fabric. "Someone here is overdressed."

"Not for long," he promised and quickly got rid of his own clothing before laying her back on the cool, soft sheets.

He looked down at her for a long minute, and Keira arched her back from the bed and stretched both hands back and over her head, enjoying the power of his gaze on her. She saw the passion in his eyes and responded, moving sinuously over the bed, sweeping her own hands down her body, pausing at her breasts, stroking her own nipples as she watched his eyes darken and his jaw clench. Finally, when she lifted both hands toward him in open invitation, Nathan groaned and leaned over her.

"No bruises," he said quietly as he studied her.

She smiled and stroked his cheek with her fingertips. "It's been a good week for me. You were always around to rescue me from a fall."

"You're making me nuts. You know that, right?"

She reached up and cupped his face between her palms. Drawing his head down to hers, she kissed him once, twice and again. "Of course I know. The question is, what're you going to do about it?"

"Return the favor," he assured her.

He kissed her, hard and long and deep, until her body was quivering and her breath was hissing from her lungs. And when she tried to hold onto him, to pull him closer, Nathan slipped from her grasp and Keira could only watch as he moved along her body, sliding his flesh across hers, kissing every inch of her skin as he moved down the length of her.

She trembled, her breath caught and she bit into her bottom lip as she moved, twisting into him, arching into his movements, trying to keep their bodies connected, their flesh burning into each other's.

But Nathan had other ideas; he continued his slow, torturous assault on her nerve endings by stroking his tongue across her abdomen and nibbling at her skin until she was whispering his name in a broken hush. He smiled against her body, and kept moving, lower and lower still until finally he had backed off the mattress.

And kneeling beside the bed, he grabbed her legs and pulled her close, until her legs hung free and she was balanced precariously on the edge of the bed. He lifted her legs, laying them across his shoulders and Keira watched him as he smiled knowingly.

"Your turn," he whispered and scooped his hands under her behind before lifting her to meet his questing mouth.

Keira sucked in a gulp of air and held it, afraid to let it out because if she did, she might not be able to draw another, and she was pretty sure she was going to need to breathe.

His mouth claimed her, and Keira pushed herself up

onto her elbows to watch him take her more intimately than anyone ever had before. Her eyes widened and locked on him, as aroused by the sight of him taking her as she was by the incredible sensations coursing through her.

Keira had never known anything like it. His tongue swept a caress across her inner folds and dipped within her body to tempt her with even more.

She was really grateful for that lungful of air, because now she had forgotten how to breathe. Her world centered on this one man and what he was doing to her body.

Again and again, he stroked and nibbled and caressed. His tongue touched a tiny bud of sensitized flesh and—" Nathan!"

She felt him smiling, and then lost herself in the wonder of what he was able to do to her. He suckled and teased and stroked until the ball of need in the pit of her stomach bubbled into a fiery cauldron that tipped and spilled an unbelievable heat throughout her body. Keira rocked her hips, reached down to cup the back of his head to hold him to her and couldn't seem to look away.

Her heels dug into his back as he slipped one finger, then two inside her body and quickened the intensity of her experience in a heartbeat. There was so much, too much. Her mind couldn't capture it all, so she quit trying and surrendered to the incredible wash of anticipation building within.

"Nathan, if you stop," she whispered through dry lips, "I'll have to kill you."

He chuckled and then closed his mouth over that one most sensitive spot. Keira cried out his name as her body shuddered with the force of the climax ripping through her. She held onto him as the only stable point in the universe and as the tremors rocking her slowly faded, like far-reaching ripples in a pond, Nathan moved, easing her legs from his shoulders, shifting her further back onto the bed and then covering her body with his own.

"I can't...I mean..." She blew out a breath and laughed shortly. "I think I may be paralyzed."

"Not yet you're not," he murmured, dipping his head to taste one of her pale-pink nipples.

Instantly, need rebuilt at the feel of his body pressing her down into the so-soft mattress. She stroked his skin, running her hands up and down his back, kissing the underside of his jaw, his neck.

"That was..." she said.

"Only the beginning," he said and kissed her, his tongue plunging into her mouth, tangling with hers, stealing what breath she had left, then giving her his own to replace it.

Keira's body lit up again with fresh need and she lifted both legs to wrap them around his waist. "I want you inside me, Nathan."

"Just where I want to be, Keira," he whispered and lifted his head so he could watch her face as he entered her.

She tipped her head back on the bed, but kept her gaze locked with his. He pushed himself home with one long, deep stroke, and Keira gasped as she rocked her hips, taking even more of him within.

Outside, the storm raged, and inside, a different kind of storm swept the two of them into a world of mindless passion. Where all that mattered was the next touch, the next kiss, the next stroke of heat to heat. Their bodies moved in an ancient dance with a rhythm that seemed as old as time and as new as her next breath.

His body moved with hers, invaded hers, claimed hers, and Keira gave him all she had to give. Her hands smoothed over his back and around to stroke down his chest, her thumbnails flicking at his flat, brown nipples until he was gritting his teeth to hold back a shout.

She liked knowing that he was as lost to sensation as she was. That his body was screaming for release as loudly as her own. That she could shatter Nathan's rigid sense of control.

Arching into him again and again, she urged him deeper, faster, harder. Her fingers clawed at his back while the pressure within tightened ferociously, demanding release.

"Now, Nathan," she groaned, moving with him at a fever pitch that couldn't be sustained without the two of them bursting into flames, "please *now.*"

He pushed himself up on his hands, stared down at her face and whispered, "You first, Keira. You first and I'll follow."

He slid one hand down the length of her body, across her flat abdomen, down to where their bodies were joined. His fingers dipped into the joining and stroked her damp heat as he continued to move inside her.

"Nathan!" Keira shrieked his name, clutched at his shoulders and bucked beneath him as an overwhelming wave of pleasure swept through her on what felt like an endless tide of mind-shattering explosions rattling just beneath her skin.

"Now," he groaned and plunged deep inside her, his

body shaking as he fell into the same tidal wave that had captured Keira and let it carry them both away.

An hour…or, for all Keira knew, a *week* later, she forced her eyelids open and stared up at the ceiling. Fire-cast shadows leaped and danced across the beams in hypnotic pulses.

"You okay?" Nathan murmured from close to her ear.

"Not sure yet," she admitted, turning her head on the pillow to smile at him. Reaching out, she smoothed his hair back from his forehead with her fingertips. "Hey, I can move my hand, so…good sign!"

Pushing himself up on one elbow, he stared down at her for a long minute or two, his eyes unreadable. A curl of unease opened inside Keira as she studied him, searching for a shadow of the passionate man he'd been so short a time ago. But the Nathan watching her now was more like the closed-off man she'd met his first day at the lodge.

"What?" she finally asked, unable to stand the silence any longer.

"I was just thinking."

"About?" she coaxed.

He looked as if he were about to say something, then thought better of it. Shaking his head, he said only, "Nothing. Never mind."

He rolled off the bed and walked naked across the room to a door that he opened to reveal a gigantic closet. It was practically empty from what Keira could see, since he'd brought only enough clothes for a month. But he stepped inside and when he came back out, he was wearing a thick black robe and carrying a dark green one that he tossed onto the foot of the bed. "I brought my own robe, but this green one was hanging in the closet when I got here."

"Thanks," she said, reaching for it and shoving both arms into the sleeves before slipping off the bed and tying the belt of the robe at her waist.

His features were tight, closed off as if he were carefully preventing whatever he was thinking from showing on his face. Which only served to really irritate Keira. A few minutes ago, they'd shared something truly amazing. They'd been as close as two people could get. Yet now…he was looking at her as if she were a stranger.

A really unwelcome stranger.

"Nathan, what's going on?"

"Not a thing," he said and started for the bedroom door and the stairs beyond. "But I promised you food, didn't I? I'll check out the kitchen. See what I can find."

Very nice, Keira thought. He'd shut her out so politely, so neatly, she had to wonder if maybe his hideous grandmother, who'd shipped him off to boarding school with hardly a wave goodbye, had taught him how to do that? How to push people away without even breaking a sweat.

Well, she wasn't going anywhere. Not until the storm stopped. And to be honest, even if the storm stopped right this minute, she wouldn't have been going anywhere. Not until she found out what the hell had happened to send Nathan from orgasmic to crabby in no time at all.

She followed him down the stairs, keeping one hand on the banister to make sure she didn't fall down the damn stairs and break her neck before she got some answers. She made a sharp right at the bottom of the stairs just in time to see his black robe disappear into the distant kitchen.

Well, if he thought she was that easy to get rid of, he really didn't know her well at all. Walking quickly, her bare feet hardly making a sound on the area rugs tossed across the gleaming wood floors, Keira got to the swinging door to the kitchen, slapped her palm against it and sent it crashing open.

He was at the fridge and raised his head to look at her when she stepped into the room. Then he dismissed her coolly, reached into the freezer and pulled out a long, flat aluminum tray.

"The housekeeper fills the freezer for me once a week. I think this is…" He read the label. "Fettuccine Alfredo with grilled garlic chicken. It's from the Clearwater, the restaurant you seem so fond of."

"Their fettuccine is great," Keira said, walking toward the granite counter and one of the stools pulled up beneath it. She sat down and tucked her bare feet up to get them off the cold floor.

"Glad you approve," he said, and turned to quickly take off the lid, turn on the oven and pop the tray inside. "Shouldn't take too long," he said, and walked to the wine cooler along the wall. "Would you like a glass of wine?"

"Sure," Keira said, trying to figure out a way to get past the wall he'd erected around himself so quickly and so completely. "Nathan, is everything all right?"

"Why wouldn't it be?"

"You're just acting a little…weird."

One black eyebrow rose as he set a bottle of white wine on the countertop. He opened a drawer, took out a corkscrew and then tore off the foil top from the bottle. Keira shivered a little and he said, "Cold?"

"A bit."

There was another fireplace in the kitchen, but this one was cold and dark. Beyond the windows leading to the covered deck, the world was a whirl of white. Light faded from the sky, the heavy clouds dropped even lower, and the flurries of snow were thick enough that it looked as though someone had hung a sheet from the edge of the patio cover.

"There's extra firewood on the deck. I'll get some."

"Okay, fine," Keira said as Nathan walked to the back door, "but first, tell me what you were going to say upstairs. When you were looking at me so funny. When you said, 'oh, it's nothing, never mind.'"

"Keira," he said with a sigh, "just let it go."

"Oh no," she assured him, shaking her head at the sheer folly of the man. "That's never gonna happen. So it'll be quicker and easier on both of us if you'll just spit it out."

"It's nothing."

"Then *say* it," she insisted.

One hand on the doorknob, he stared at her for a long moment, as if trying to decide whether to speak or not. At last, though, he nodded and said, "Fine. I was thinking about the sex. And I wondered just how far you were willing to go to get me to stay here for the whole month."

Keira felt the slap of his words like a physical blow. Stung, humiliated and furious, she glared at him with enough heat that, if there were any justice at all, he would have been a pillar of fire. "Are you serious?"

"You asked what I was going to say," he said and watched her through narrowed eyes.

"I didn't know you were going to say *that!*"

"Don't sound so offended." Nathan looked at her for a long minute. "It's not like I'm surprised."

"Is that right?"

"For God's sake, Keira, you think this is the first time a woman's used her body to get me to do something for her? We're both adults. You wanted something from me and you used sex to get it."

Fury whipped through Keira. "You…you…"

He shrugged and headed for the back door. "It was good for both of us. We each got what we wanted. No point now in trying to make it something it wasn't."

He opened the back door to a gust of icy wind and said, "Look, let's just forget it, all right?"

"Sure," she whispered as she watched him hurry barefoot across the icy deck toward the neatly stacked pile of firewood. As he gathered up a few logs and some kindling, the wind whipping the edges of his robe around his calves, Keira jumped off her stool, crossed the floor and quietly closed and locked the back door.

Instantly he straightened up, whirled around and shocked, stared at her through the glass. He crossed to the door and gave the knob a turn and a shake. "Keira, open the damn door."

"I don't think so," she said, folding her arms over her chest and tapping one bare foot against the cold wood floor.

She'd never been so mad in her whole life. *Or* so humiliated. For God's sake, she'd let him do things to her no one had ever done before, only because she'd felt a connection to him somehow. Some minuscule, apparently clearly one-sided, *feeling.* How could he ever think that she would have slept with him just to make him stay?

Did she really give off such a slutty vibe?

And what the hell kind of people was he so used to dealing with that would make him assume she was so coldblooded?

He shivered, clutched the firewood tighter to his chest and gave her a glare she was sure sent his employees scuttling for cover.

Keira, however, remained unmoved.

"Damn it, Keira, it's snowing out here!"

"You're under the porch roof."

"It's freezing."

"Start a fire."

"On the *deck?*"

"Frankly, I don't care if you freeze solid to the spot. I'll put up a small but tasteful plaque, something like Here Stands An American Moron."

"This is *not* funny!" he shouted, and hunched deeper into his way-too-thin-for-snow robe.

"No kidding!" Keira walked closer to the glass so she could burn her stare into his eyes. "I cannot believe you. You actually think I'd *prostitute* myself to get you to stay here?"

"I didn't say *that*," he reasoned.

"Oh, yes you did, you pompous, self important, miserable son of a bitch."

"Look, I was *wrong*, okay?"

"You're just saying that so I'll open the door," she snapped.

"Damn straight."

"Well, forget it! You deserve to freeze, but you

probably won't. You're so damn cold already, I don't see how you could possibly get any colder!"

"Can you let me the hell in the house and *then* yell at me?"

"Why should I let you in?" she demanded, so furious she was seeing red at the edges of her vision. Amazing. You really *did* see red if you were angry enough.

"Because…because…"

"See? Even *you* can't think of a reason!" Keira shouted.

"Hah!" Nathan raised one hand in the air, dropped some kindling on his foot and hopped in place. "Because if I die out here, I won't be able to stay the damn month and your town won't get the money you want so badly."

"Funny," she said, thoughtfully tapping one finger against her chin, "but I don't remember it saying anywhere in the will that you had to be *alive* and here for a month. It'd probably be okay if we just prop you up out there on the deck."

"You are the most infuriating woman I have ever met."

"You've got a heck of a lot of nerve, Nathan Barrister. You call me a *ho,* and I'm the one who's infuriating?"

He flicked a glance behind him when the wind shifted and a flurry of snow rushed at him from the lake. Turning his gaze back to hers, he said tightly, "Keira, open this damn door and let me inside."

"And if I don't?"

"Then I'll break the glass with one of these logs and we'll *both* be freezing our asses off."

Hmm. Good point. Well, she hadn't really planned on letting him become an ice sculpture on the deck. Though the idea was all too tempting at the moment.

"Fine." She reached out, unlocked the door and then stomped across the room so she was as far from Nathan as she could get and still be able to give him dirty looks.

He rushed into the room, dropped the firewood into the hearth, then pounded his bare feet against the floor and slapped his hands at his arms, trying to get his blood moving.

"Cold?" she asked sweetly.

"Funny," he snapped, snarling at her.

"As cold as that tiny little marble in your chest? You know, the one you call your *heart?*"

Still shivering, he turned his back on her, started a fire in the hearth and huddled next to the flames as they sputtered, caught and licked at the dry wood. Finally, he turned a look on her. "My heart's got nothing to do with any of this."

"Since it probably gets very little use, I'm willing to bet you're right," Keira hissed.

"You tried to freeze me to death!" His voice ricocheted off the high beamed ceiling and Keira didn't even flinch.

"Don't be such a baby."

"A *baby?*" Astonishment flashed across his features and she waved one hand at him dismissively.

"You're lucky I let you back in."

There was a long moment of silence before he finally said, "Yeah. You're just crazy enough to have left me out there, so I guess I am lucky. And frostbitten."

"That was a nasty thing to think about me," she said, ignoring his complaint, "and even nastier to say."

"You wouldn't leave it alone. You had to know what I was thinking," he pointed out, raising his hands high in amazement. "What is it about women, anyway? They poke and prod at a man to tell them what he's thinking and when he does, they lock him outside in a damn snowstorm!"

"Is it our fault that what you're really thinking is so ridiculously insulting that we aren't prepared?" Keira slapped the granite counter. "We want to know what you're thinking, because, silly us, we actually think your minds *aren't* twisted little black holes."

"No, you expect us to be like you," Nathan said tightly, still scowling, still stamping his feet on the floor trying to get his circulation moving again. "All warm and fuzzy, wanting kids and a dog and a white picket fence and—"

"Are you *delusional?*" Keira interrupted his rant. "Who said anything about a picket fence?"

"You don't have to say it," he challenged, stabbing one finger in the air, pointed at her. "It's who you are. You're Ms. Roots herself. Well, I don't have roots. Don't want any and if I found some I'd rip 'em out of the ground."

Keira stomped across the room until she was right in front of him. His blue eyes were wild and hot, and the set of his jaw told her he was every bit as furious as she was. Well, good. No point in being mad all by yourself. And besides, he'd probably *never* lost his temper. Not the ever-polite, always distant Nathan Barrister. So, she'd let him rant and rave. Maybe it'd do him some good. God knows it was doing wonders for *her.*

"Your perfect little town has nothing I want or need. As soon as possible, I'll be on my jet, heading for the opposite end of the world."

"Good. Nobody's asking you to settle down in

Hunter's Landing, *Mr. Wonderful*." Keira stabbed her finger at him, poking him several times dead center of the chest until he grabbed her finger in self defense. She shook him off a second later. "*I'm* certainly not laying out traps for you—"

"Oh, no?" Nathan countered quickly, apparently enjoying interrupting her for a change. "No traps, huh? Did it happen to escape your notice that we didn't use any protection?"

Keira blanched for a second. Damn it, it *had* escaped her attention. Then his words hit home. *A trap?* "First I'm a slut and now I'm trying to trap you and your golden sperm? Aren't I the busy little bee?"

"You're deliberately avoiding the point," he said. "We didn't use anything and—"

"Well, jeez," she said, interrupting him neatly for the umpteenth time, "color me *human*. You know, I don't actually travel with condoms in my jeans on the off chance that some spoiled, snotty rich guy will want to have sex with me and then insult me!"

He grabbed two fists full of his own hair and yanked. Hard. Then, his voice rumbled through the kitchen at a level just below howling. "For God's sake, I just told you I could have made you pregnant and you take *that* as an insult, too?"

"I'm not pregnant," she snapped. "Just so you know, I'm on the Pill, so no worries there, Mr. Barrister. Your personal fortune is safe from this particular gold digger."

"I never said you were a—"

"But as long as we're on the subject," she continued, her voice rolling right over his, "how about you?"

He grimaced. "I'm not on the Pill."

"Not the best time to develop a sense of humor, just so you know."

He raised his hands in mock surrender. "Fine. Fine. I'm healthy. No worries there. You?"

"Contrary to certain people's opinion, I am *not* a slut and, therefore, I, too, am very healthy." She crossed her fingers over her heart. "Of course, I'll be happy to get you a letter from my doctor to alleviate any further concern…"

"Damn it, Keira, I'm not calling you a slut for doing whatever you have to do to get what you want. That's how the world works. The real world, that is, not your own personal little Xanadu here."

"Believe it or not," she shouted, "I did *not* have sex with you to keep you here for the month!"

"You keep telling yourself that," he said tightly.

"Jeez," Keira muttered, shaking her head. "Are you really so far out of touch with humanity? Does *everything* in your world carry a price tag?"

"There are price tags everywhere in the world. Wake up and maybe you'll notice them."

"You lead an ugly life," she whispered.

"At least I live with my eyes open," he countered. "I know that people are mostly out for themselves and willing to do just about anything to take care of number one."

"So I slept with you to get what I want?"

"Wouldn't be the first time it's happened."

Keira flinched at the coldness in his eyes. He really did believe that anyone getting close to him was out for his money. His lifestyle. How sad. How unbearably empty his world must be. And the saddest part was, he didn't even realize it.

"And so, because you've surrounded yourself with

sycophants and users, you naturally assumed that I was one, too."

He gritted his teeth and a muscle in his jaw twitched. "And you're telling me you're not."

"Yeah," she said, "I am. And what's more, you know it. Somewhere in that cavernous emptiness you call a heart, you know it. And you insulted me on purpose."

He glared at her. "You are the most—" He caught himself, dragged in a gulp of air and then fired his gaze into hers. "Okay, yeah. I did."

"Finally!" Keira shouted and scooted a little closer to the kitchen fire, nudging Nathan out of her way. "The question is *why?*"

"Why?"

"Why did you want to insult me, Nathan?" She tipped her head to one side, stared up at him and asked, "If you wanted me to leave, all you had to do was say so."

"I didn't want you to leave," he admitted, though it was clear he wasn't happy about the confession.

"Then why?"

"I honestly don't know," he said and pulled her up close against him. When she tried to push herself free, he simply tightened his hold on her middle, pinning her body to his until Keira could feel his need building again.

Was he so unused to people wanting to be with him just to be with him? Was his world so insulated that the only people he ever saw were the ones who worked for him or wanted something from him?

Slightly mollified, Keira stared up into his eyes and saw questions still lingering in those pale blue depths. The man did things to her she had never expected. He had a way of touching her heart at the oddest moments and she was more than a little confused about that.

She could continue the fight, which, let's face it, she was enjoying. She could give him answers to his questions. She could even make him wonder about lots of other things.

Or, she could do what she most wanted to do.

Tugging the lapels of his thick, cashmere robe aside, Keira stroked his bare chest with the flat of her palms and watched his eyes narrow into slits and his jaw clench as he hissed in a long, slow breath.

Deliberately, she teased him, spreading his robe open, baring his body to her touch. She slid her hands over his still cold skin and felt heat bubble beneath the surface at her touch. Then she tugged the belt of the robe free and swept one hand down to capture his hard length in a soft, firm grip.

"You know, Nathan," she said, smoothing her fingers up and down his erection with slow caresses, "the simple truth is, I've wanted you almost from the moment I first saw you. That's why I stayed. That's why I want you again now."

He groaned as she slipped her free hand down to cup him. "Works for me."

Eight

The rich scent of Alfredo sauce was beginning to fill the kitchen, but Keira was hungry for something other than food. Strange, but even fighting with Nathan was stimulating.

Her body was quickening as his hands moved to tug her robe open and pull it down off her shoulders to let it pool on the floor at her feet. The air in the kitchen was still icy from the wind that had whooshed inside when the door was opened. Yet she didn't really mind it. Instead, that sensation added to the others already coursing through her body, mingling together, causing a ripple effect of near turmoil in her system.

His hands swept up and down her body, his long, talented fingers exploring every curve as she ran her own hands over him. His broad, muscular chest was clearly defined, sculpted and tanned, making him look as though he were carved from the same kind of honey-toned wood that graced the lodge.

But he was warm and ready, and his body was already pressing into hers, letting her know that he felt the same blood pounding need she did.

"Why do I want you so much?" he whispered, his fingers stroking, sliding down her body to caress the heat between her thighs.

Keira sighed and swayed unsteadily on her feet as a rush of something delicious began to build within. "Why do you ask so many questions?" she answered.

He smiled, and her heart flipped in her chest. A weird sensation, but a shockingly good one.

"You're the one with all the questions," he murmured, dipping his head to kiss the curve of her neck, to nibble at the base of her throat.

Her hands moved to his shoulders and she clung to him desperately as he continued to smooth his fingers over her damp heat. Instinctively, he found that one most-sensitive bud and concentrated his attentions on it, thumb and forefinger gliding, stroking until Keira's blood felt as if it were boiling just beneath her skin.

"No questions," she said, licking dry lips and trying to catch her breath. "Not now, anyway."

He slid one hand up to hold the back of her neck while his other hand continued to gently torture her with anticipation. His blue eyes caught hers and Keira wished she knew what he was thinking now. Now, when passion simmered in pale eyes gone dark with desire.

She wanted to give him what he was giving her, so she slid one hand down his body until she could encircle his length with her fingers again. He swallowed a great gulp of air before lowering his head to take her mouth with his. His tongue plunged into her mouth, claiming her fiercely, desperately, as if he couldn't wait another moment to taste her.

And Keira matched his need with her own. She shifted position, sliding her hands around his waist to splay them against his back. She felt his heart pounding and knew her own was in sync that wild rhythm.

His fingers dipped into her center, first one, then two, diving in and out of her heat, touching her deeply, but not deep enough. Not as deeply as she wanted him. Needed him.

When he tore his mouth from hers, he stared down at her and whispered, "We'll never make it back up to the bedroom."

"Not a chance," she agreed, already so hungry for him, her arms and legs were trembling.

"Here then," he said and, moving quickly, he picked her up, carried her to the counter and plopped her down onto it.

"Yikes!" The cold granite bit into her heated skin and sent a chill slicing right through her.

He grinned wickedly. "Cold?"

She narrowed her eyes on him. "You enjoyed that. Payback for locking you outside?"

"Just a little," he admitted, then leaned in and bit her bottom lip gently, swiping his tongue along the crease in her mouth. "But I'm willing to warm you up again, too."

She reached for him, sliding her arms around his neck, pulling him in closer. "A generous man," she said with a sigh as his mouth came down on hers.

As he kissed her, he parted her thighs, moved in close and entered her body on a rush of sensation that poured through the two of them, linking them in a way that neither had experienced or expected.

Keira arched into him, moving her hips on the hard granite in a desperate attempt to get closer, to take him more fully within. She closed her eyes and saw swirls of vibrant color as her body leaped into life. Her being soared, and something deep within her unexpectedly awoke. Her eyes opened again as that thought sang through her mind. She watched him and felt new feelings stir within. New emotions. New and incredibly fragile threads of connection.

Nathan's hands dropped to her hips and he held her still, trapped within his steely grip as he plunged in and out of her depths in a ferocious rhythm designed to drive them both quickly over the edge.

The world dropped away and it was just the two of them. Nothing beyond existed anymore. Passion swelled and trapped them in a silky web of desire. Keira held on to him, and lost herself in his strength, surrendering to the twist of anticipation curling inside her.

Her body tightened, her mouth mated with his and she hooked her legs around Nathan's waist, pulling him in harder, deeper. She felt his body's invasion of hers all the way to her soul and knew she would never get enough of him. Knew that this man was touching more than her body. He'd already laid claim to a piece of her heart.

Whether she wanted it or not, she cared for him. More than she wanted to think about. More than she dared to admit.

She pulled free of his kiss so she could watch his

eyes as he claimed her. His beautiful blue gaze locked with hers, as though he understood her silent plea and felt the same way.

Her body quickened, anticipation exploded and a climax stronger than anything she'd ever known before shattered inside her, splintering itself into brilliant colors that tore through her heart and spilled into her bones.

Nathan kept his gaze fixed on hers and when she cried out his name, he gave himself up to the release clamoring inside him and followed her over the ragged edge of control, into oblivion.

By morning, Nathan was rethinking the whole situation.

The night before, he'd thought it a great idea having Keira stay with him. They'd come together often during the night and each time had been more incredible than the first. He felt as though each time he touched her, he felt something more, something different. And he'd reveled in their time together, knowing that in the morning, she would be going home.

At least, that's what he had thought.

He gritted his teeth and stared out the bank of windows in the kitchen. Outside the lodge, the world was a wash of white. Snow piled on the sides of the deck and blew in under the overhang to coat the wood planks with a layer of snow at least a foot deep. And that was under the porch roof. It was much deeper everywhere else, and it was still falling.

He'd never seen anything like it.

"It's mid-March and it looks like Siberia in December out there," he muttered.

Keira came up behind him, threaded her arms around his waist and rested her cheek against his back. "Welcome to the high Sierras."

"I tried the phone," he said. "No dial tone."

"Uh-oh."

"What's that mean?" He turned his head to look at her.

"It means," she said, "that with the phone lines down this early in the storm, it's a big one."

Nathan glowered at her. "Which translates into…?"

She shrugged. "If the roads aren't completely blocked already, they soon will be."

"Surely you have crews to take care of that."

"Of course we do," Keira said, smiling up at him. "But they can't roll till the heavy snows are over, and even when they do…"

He didn't like the look on her face. The look that said *he's not going to like this.*

"*What?*"

"They take care of the town first and then the main stretches of highway. Those are priorities for obvious reasons."

"And…?"

"And," she said with another shrug, "the roads up here probably won't be cleared for a few days."

"A few *days?*"

"Maybe sooner," she said, he suspected simply to placate him. "But the private roads and the roads leading to them are pretty much a lower priority. Unless there's an emergency or something. If the road crews get a call like that, they'll come right away."

"*The phones are out.*" He paused, then said, "Wait. I've got my satellite phone."

"But no one else around here has one."

"Right." Nathan shook his head.

She pulled her arms from around his waist, shoved her hands into the pockets of her robe and said, "Look, we do the best we can. And people generally privately contract to get their roads cleared, so that takes care of a lot of problems."

"And does the lodge have a private contract?"

"I don't know."

"Perfect." Nathan blew out a breath. This month was turning into a real trial. "How long is this going to keep up?" He shook his head as he shifted his gaze across the lake, watching snow slide in sideways, riding a wind that was rattling the windows.

"Well," she said, giving him a brilliant smile, "if it keeps up, at least it won't be coming down anymore."

He glanced at her. "Oh, very humorous."

She moved to stand in front of him, leaning both palms against an icy window to get as good a view as she could of the blustering storm outside. "I always laughed when my dad said it." She glanced at him over her shoulder. "Of course, I was ten."

Nathan wasn't amused. Nor was he charmed. He'd wanted her here last night—and he'd enjoyed every minute of his time with her. But that didn't mean he wanted her at the lodge for freaking *ever.* Scowling, he saw the wind spit snow at the windows and knew that she wouldn't be going anywhere. At least not today.

As if she was reading his mind, Keira turned around, leaned back against the floor-to-ceiling windows and tipped her head to one side, staring up at him. "So, what'll we do while we're stuck inside?"

He knew that gleam in her eye. Hell, he'd seen it most of the night. He was willing to bet they hadn't had more than a couple of hours' sleep. Yet even thinking about being inside her, touching her, holding her, tasting her, made him hard and eager again.

Which was clearly unacceptable.

He wasn't a kid to be led around by his groin. And damned if he'd let himself get any more tangled up with Keira than he already was. Just because she was here, with him, didn't mean she had to be *with* him.

"Uh-oh," she said, tugging the edges of her robe more firmly together over her chest. "It suddenly got very cold in here."

He nodded. "I'll turn up the thermostat."

"That's not what I meant."

"What're you talking about?" he asked as he walked to the coffee pot on the kitchen counter.

God.

The counter.

How was he ever supposed to walk through this kitchen again without remembering her sitting naked on that counter? Without thinking about how she'd taken him so deep inside her he'd thought he might never find his way out again?

Crap.

Now he had a headache.

Rubbing his temple, he asked, "Coffee?"

"Sure. I'll have a cup of coffee, black, with answers."

"Huh?" He half turned to look at her as she walked slowly across the kitchen. Did her hips always sway like that, he wondered, or was she doing it purposely now?

"I said I'd like some answers."

"To what?" He was stalling. He knew it. He poured two cups of coffee, handed her one, then stalled again by taking a long sip of his own.

"To why your eyes suddenly looked even colder than this stormy day outside."

"Keira," he said tightly, "you're making too much of nothing."

"So you're *happy* I'm here," she coaxed, taking a drink of her coffee and moving in closer to him.

"Delirious," he assured her.

"Liar."

"Why do you do that? Accuse me of lying at every opportunity?"

"A better question is why am I always right?"

He set his coffee cup down, tugged at the belt of his robe and said, "You're not right. Women always say that to win an argument, but it's never true."

"Of course it is," Keira said, sipping her coffee. "Women are right because we *see* everything and we *remember* everything."

"Sure."

"Just like I can see that you're trying to start a fight so you won't have to answer my question."

He sighed. This woman got to him like no one else ever had. And he was forced to admit that part of the reason why was because she never took any of his crap. She always called him on everything.

"Fine," he said tightly and met her gaze with a hard look designed to put some distance between them. "I was thinking that it would be more comfortable if you could have gone home this morning. Happy?"

"Delirious," she said, throwing his own word back at

him. Then she turned around and pulled a chair out from under the kitchen table. Curling one leg under herself, she plopped down, propped her elbow on the table and took another sip of coffee before saying, "Was that so hard?"

Nathan just blinked at her. Any other woman would have been insulted, giving him all kinds of frosty attitude right now. Figured Keira would react differently. She had to everything else.

"You're not mad."

"Nope, sorry to disappoint." She took long drink of her coffee, then set the cup onto the table. "Nathan, I know you don't really want me here, and that's okay. I mean, I hadn't planned on staying forever, you know."

"Yeah, I know."

"But it's really storming out there, so I'm stuck here and you're stuck with me. We might as well make the best of it, don't you think?"

A constant surprise. Keira Sanders never failed to bewilder him with her reactions to things. He couldn't depend on what she'd do next, because she never responded to *anything* the way he expected her to. How was a man supposed to find his emotional footing if a woman kept changing on him?

"I suppose that's logical."

"Excellent," she said. "I've got a few ideas on what we could do today." She hopped off her chair, stumbled over her own foot and slammed into his chest. She grabbed him in self-preservation and spilled his coffee down the front of his robe. Grinning up at him, she said, "Maybe we should do some laundry first."

* * *

Cold fettuccine Alfredo for breakfast, a load of wash done and in the dryer, and the snow was still blowing outside.

Keira wandered through the lodge, peeking into closets and exploring rooms that were still standing empty waiting for the decorator. From every room, the view was outstanding and displayed the growing storm to its advantage.

She chewed at her bottom lip and wondered how the town was doing, then reminded herself that the people of Hunter's Landing dealt with snowstorms every year. The only difference with this storm was that she wasn't there. She couldn't see for herself that everyone was fine, hunkered down to wait out the snow.

She couldn't even *call* anyone to check on them. The phone lines were still down. Remembering the look on Nathan's face when he'd tried the phone again an hour ago made her smile.

Leaving one of the bedrooms, she wandered back into the upper hall, passed the master bedroom and paused for a moment, remembering everything she and Nathan had done together the night before. Her heart filled, her body ached with tired satisfaction and the small smile on her face faded slowly. She knew that today, he was regretting their time together.

He probably wasn't used to facing his nighttime bed partner the next day. Well, this was pretty new for Keira, too. But at least she was trying to make the best of it. Unlike Nathan, who'd buried himself in busywork on his laptop. The man had avoided talking to her for hours now and the quiet—except for his fingers hitting the keyboard—was starting to really bother her.

The wind howled around the corners of the house, sounding as though it was looking for a way in. Shivering, Keira headed for the stairs. She held onto the banister, and started down, her bare feet making no sound at all on the dark carpet runner that covered the wood planks.

Walking into the great room, she headed for the fire crackling in the hearth, turned her back to it and stared at Nathan, just a few feet away. He hadn't even looked up when she entered the room.

"Ignoring me doesn't make me invisible," she said abruptly.

"Huh? What?" He raised his head, turned to look at her and asked, "What did you say?"

"I said, are you going to be sitting in front of that computer all day?"

"I have work to do."

"That you can't send anywhere because the phone lines are down."

"It's not e-mail, it's work," he said.

"Fine." She blew out a breath, walked toward him, then squatted beside him until they were eye to eye. "My point is, does *everything* have to be done *today?*"

"Keira…"

She hopped up, plopped onto the couch beside him and leaned in, staring at the computer screen. "Okay, okay. So you have to work. Tell me about it. Talk to me."

He sighed in resignation, and Keira hid a smile. "I'm working up a new schedule for impromptu visits to my hotels."

She looked at him, stupefied for a second, then burst out laughing.

"What's so funny?"

She waved one hand, shook her head and fought for breath. Laughter spilled from her throat, bubbled into the room and crashed down around them as she wrapped her arms around his shoulders and gave him a fast hug. "Nathan, you're really something," she said when she finally got control of her giggles.

"I'm so happy I can entertain you."

"Don't you get it?" she asked, grinning. "You're making a *schedule* for *impromptu* visits. The whole point of impromptu is *no* schedule."

Nathan scowled at her, then at the computer screen. He felt like an idiot. But in his own defense, he'd only been making busy work anyway. Anything to keep his mind off the fact that Keira was here and way too accessible.

He had no intention of getting in any deeper with her. And the best way to keep from doing that was to keep his hands to himself. Yet…everytime he heard her breathe, or caught a whiff of her scent, all he wanted to do was carry her back upstairs and bury himself inside her.

He wanted to experience again that incredible warmth that he'd only found with her. But it wouldn't be right. He wanted to enjoy her, enjoy their time together and still be able to walk away. Because he *would* be leaving. Nothing would stop him.

She reached out and closed the computer, then clambered onto his lap. Threading her arms around his neck, she looked into his eyes and asked, "What do you do when you're not working?"

He didn't have an answer. Strange, but he'd never really thought about it. "I'm always working."

"Well, let's see what we can do about that."

Nine

An hour later, Nathan rolled out of bed, his body replete, his mind racing. He glanced at Keira languidly stretching on the mattress and had to fight down an urge to lay back down and gather her up close. And because that thought was uppermost in his brain, he took a step or two away from the bed just for good measure.

"Now," she said, sweeping her hair up to lay across the pillow like a red-gold banner, "wasn't that more fun than planning schedules?"

He grabbed his robe from the end of the bed, slipped it on, then stood up to look down at her. "If we spend the next few days like this," he said with a smile he couldn't quite prevent curving his mouth, "by the time the storm ends, we'll be dead."

"I can think of worse ways to go."

So could he. That was one of his problems. Always before, Nathan's relationships with women had been uncomplicated and straightforward. Before he took a woman to bed, he made sure she felt as he did about affairs—that they should be undemanding, easily slipped in and out of, with no hard feelings, no promises made, so no promises broken.

Ordinarily, he never would have become involved with a woman like Keira. She had "complications" written all over her. And yet, at this moment, he couldn't really bring himself to regret what he'd found with her.

Regrets would come later. Once he was gone and safely wrapped up in his normal world. Once he was far enough away from her eyes that they didn't haunt him every damn minute.

"You're an unusual woman."

She sat up, completely comfortable with her own nudity, and swung her hair back from her face. "Thanks."

"You're welcome," he said, his gaze dipping to the swell of her breasts, then back to her fathomless green eyes. She was tempting. More tempting than anyone he'd ever known before. He was walking through unfamiliar territory here and he felt as though he were trying to negotiate his way through quicksand.

What he needed was a little space. A little time to himself to gather his defenses and shore up the inner walls she seemed so determine to shatter.

Decision made, he said, "I'm going downstairs to get some work done."

She looked at him for a long second or two, shook her head, then flopped back onto the bed, dragged the quilt up to cover herself and muttered, "Of course you are."

* * *

A few hours later, Nathan was hunched determinedly over his computer, doing an excellent job of pretending Keira wasn't in the room.

Tossing the book she'd been trying to read for the last half hour onto the sofa cushion beside her, she frowned at the back of his head and said pointedly, "What're you doing?"

"Working."

"*Again,* you mean. Well, I can see that, Mr. Chatty. Working on what? Still trying to find a way to schedule spontaneity?"

"No." He shook his head, turned back to the computer and typed something else.

"Then what?"

"You're not going to give me any peace at all, are you?"

"Probably not," she said.

"Fine." He leaned back into the couch, winced and retrieved the book she'd dropped out from behind his back and set it on the coffee table. When he was settled again, he glanced at her and said, "I'm making some notes on how to confront the manager of the Gstaad Barrister."

"Switzerland," she said with a sigh. Then she asked, "Confront? About what?"

"I gave him specific instructions last time on how I wanted him to deal with the housekeeping staff, and they haven't been implemented."

"Why not?"

He looked at her. "How the hell do I know?"

She curled her legs up under her, propped her elbow on the back of the sofa and leaned in. "What's wrong with the way *he's* handling things, then?"

Nathan sighed. "He's very…relaxed in his position. He allows the employees too much leeway in their work."

"Does it all get done?"

"Yes, but—"

"So maybe," Keira said, "he knows his people better than you do?"

"Maybe, but—"

She smiled. "So if you weren't stomping around bellowing orders like a bully, maybe you'd get more cooperation out of him?"

"I do *not* bellow," Nathan said and sat up straight.

"But you *do* bully."

He blew out a disgusted breath. "You don't understand. There's a right way and a wrong way to run a business, Keira."

"Oh, I understand," she said, reaching out to pat his shoulder, then letting her fingertips linger there just a moment or two. "Believe me, as mayor, I have to deal with people all the time. And it's just not logical to assume you can use the same strategy when dealing with different types of people."

"It's always worked before," he pointed out, scowling at her.

Keira scooted closer, leaned down and looked him dead in the eye. This she knew about. He might own all of the gorgeous hotels in the world, but Nathan Barrister was *not* a people person.

"But the thing is, Nathan, you don't know if it might work better doing things differently."

"The company's policy has been in effect since my grandfather started the first hotel."

"Jeez," she said softly. "No wonder it's out-of-date."

"I didn't say it was out-of-date."

"Nope. I did." Turning around, she sat back beside Nathan, tucked her hand through the crook of his arm and cuddled in. "Like, for instance, when Donna—she owns the pottery shop on the outskirts of town—wanted to increase her number of parking spaces in front of her shop, I went to bat for her with the town council. After all, her shop is out of the way, it wouldn't infringe on anyone else's parking. Why not?"

"Okay…"

"But, when the Clearwater wanted the same deal, I had to tell them no. Because they're in the middle of town, lakeside, and we just couldn't afford to lose tourist parking slots to make more room for their customers. Different situations, different rules."

"Ah," he said, smiling at her, "but the situations in my hotels are all the same. Each one is a Barrister. So the rules should apply evenly."

She nudged his shoulder and laughed shortly. "The hotels are all in different places. Different traditions, different employees."

"But—"

"Would you decorate your Barbados hotel the same way you decorated the one in say, D.C.?"

"No…"

"So, same thing applies." Leaning her head against his shoulder, she added, "Cut your managers a little slack, Nathan. Trust them to know their people and their hotels. Lighten up a little and you might be surprised by the results you get."

He frowned thoughtfully and shifted his gaze to the screen of his laptop, where his carefully written-up notes were marked with bullet points. "You couldn't have made your point an hour ago? Before I started working on this stupid list?"

Keira laughed and Nathan took a heartbeat of time to simply enjoy the sound as it swirled around him. She was cuddled in close and he liked the feel of her pressed against him. He liked knowing she was sitting beside him reading quietly—or that she was in the kitchen making grilled cheese sandwiches—or tripping over a rug on her way down the hall.

He just liked knowing she was here. Outside, the storm was still blowing and Nathan was willing to admit, at least to himself, that if he had been here, trapped by himself, he would have been half crazy by now.

But having her here made for a different sort of crazy. Keira was becoming too much a part of his world. He hated knowing that he was beginning to count on hearing her move through the house. That he was looking forward to their next argument. That he wanted her even more now than he had the first time they were together.

Somehow, she was worming her way right into the heart of him. And Nathan wasn't sure how to keep her at a distance anymore. Or even if he wanted to. Which worried him more than a little.

He hadn't thought about anything but business for years. Now, his life was on hold and he was in a situation where the rules had all changed on him. He was in a place where there was too little work to do and too few distractions to keep him from having too much time to think. To wonder. To ask himself a few fundamental questions. Like what his life might have been like if he'd taken a different path.

He supposed most men wondered those things from time to time, but he never had. He'd never had any doubts about his life or how he lived it.

Until now.

Until Keira.

"What're you thinking?" she asked.

"No way," he said. "I'm not playing that game again. I'm in no mood to get frostbite, thanks."

Keira laughed, gave him a punch on the arm and said, "Fine, coward. Can I use your satellite phone?"

He turned and looked at her, curiosity taking small, annoying bites of him. "Who're you going to call? The lines are all down, remember?"

"My sister," Keira said. "I know, it's really long distance, you know, to London and all. But I won't stay on long and I'll pay for the call."

Something inside him eased back and he really didn't want to explore what that might mean. Instead, he rummaged through the briefcase beside him on the floor, came up with the phone and handed it over. "Talk as long as you want. My treat."

"Wow. You'll do *anything* to get me to leave you alone, huh?"

The answer to that question should have been yes. Since he wasn't sure anymore if it was or not, he said nothing, just turned back to his computer and began to delete his well-thought-out letter.

Keira punched in her sister's number as she walked into the kitchen and poured herself a cup of coffee.

While she waited for Kelly to pick up, she took a sip and leaned back against the kitchen counter.

"Hello?"

"Hey, Kel," Keira said, pushing away from the counter and walking toward the bank of windows. Her gaze fixed on the storm still blowing like crazy out there, she listened to Kelly's excited yelp and settled in for a good talk.

"Where have you *been?*" Kelly demanded. "I've been trying to get you forever but the phone at home's out of order and, by the way, how are you calling me and whose phone is it? I didn't recognize the number."

Keira laughed, took another sip of hot coffee and said, "Big storm blew in yesterday. Phone lines are down."

"Then how—"

"It's a satellite phone," Keira said quickly. "Nathan let me borrow it."

"*Nathan,* is it?" Kelly whistled a little, then asked, "what's he doing at the house?"

"He's not at the house, *Mom*—I'm at his place."

"You mean the lodge?"

"That's the one." Keira grinned and watched her reflection smile back at her.

"So this storm. How bad is it?"

"Phone lines down, remember?"

"Which means the roads are blocked, which means you're stranded in that big lodge with Nathan Barrister?"

Keira laughed. "All that college wasn't a waste after all. You're really quick."

"Very funny. How did this happen? Oh, K. You slept with him, didn't you?"

"Kelly…" Keira glanced back over her shoulder, as if Nathan could hear her sister's voice.

"You did. I can *so* hear it in your tone. It's that, *this is none of your business, butt out, Kelly,* tone. I know it well."

"And yet," Keira said through gritted teeth, "you always seem to ignore it."

"I'm sorry. No, wait. I'm not. Honest to God, Keira, are you nuts? This is Nathan Barrister, for God's sake. He is sooooooo not your type."

A quick jolt of anger shot through Keira but she managed to squelch it before she could shout. "What exactly *is* my type then, Kel? You tell me."

"Someone remotely normal? As in, not some damn recluse? Someone who isn't one of the richest men on the planet? Someone who isn't *renowned* for strings of one night stands?"

Well, Keira thought bitterly, she'd had to ask. "You're really making me sorry I called," she muttered and took another drink of coffee, appreciating the scalding heat as it sang down her throat.

"It's not like I don't want you to find somebody," Kelly said, her voice a lot softer now, as if carrying an apology she wouldn't actually say, "it's just. Keira, you've been down this road before, remember? Remember how hurt you were?"

"Trust me," Keira said tightly. "I remember."

How in the hell could she forget? Three years ago, she'd fallen madly, wildly in love with an Olympic skier who was in town training over the winter. Max had been exciting and funny and sexy and he had seemed to care for her as much as she had for him.

In a few short months, they had gotten so close that Keira was mentally making plans for a life together.

They spent every night locked in each other's arms. And Keira had never been so happy.

She'd never seen him for what he really was. Never suspected that he didn't feel the same way she did.

Until the day his fiancée rolled into town.

And Max, smooth, gorgeous Max, had turned and introduced Keira to the woman he was going to marry— as a *"good friend."*

The pain of that humiliation was going to be with her forever. Seeing the sympathetic understanding in the other woman's eyes when they met had told Keira that she wasn't the first woman he'd cheated with. Wasn't the first woman he'd lied to.

But that information had done little to heal a broken heart.

So, when the aching misery had finally faded along with her memories, Keira had made herself a promise. To protect herself, she wasn't going to fall for anyone again. Wouldn't believe more pretty lies. Wouldn't let a man get so deep inside her that she couldn't shake him loose any time she wanted to.

And her plan had worked pretty well. Until Nathan Barrister had walked into her life. Now she knew that her sister was right to worry. Because Keira was falling for him.

Despite knowing better, despite knowing that there was no future for them, her heart hadn't learned its lesson.

"I know you remember," Kelly said softly. "And I don't want to hurt you. It's just…I don't want to see you get all torn up again."

"Kelly…"

"Keira, why don't you come to London? Right now.

Well, okay, when the storm stops. Hop on a plane and come see me. It'll give you some distance. Some time to think. And you've been promising for a year you'd come anyway."

"I can't," Keira said, leaning her forehead against the window, allowing the icy cold to sweep through her. "I can't just pack up and go. You know that."

"I know that the town would be just fine without you for a month. Or two."

Chuckling in spite of the heaviness in her heart, Keira said, "Two months? Oh, I'm sure Tony would love to have your big sister around for that long. Great idea, Kel."

"Omigod!"

"What?" Keira's heart jolted. "What is it?"

"Tony. I can't believe I forgot."

"Is he okay?" Keira asked, though she couldn't imagine that her little sister would have had time to lecture her about her love life if her own man were in danger.

"Oh, he's way better than okay," Kelly said, then without even taking a breath, continued in a rush. "Remember I told you he was taking me to Paris for the weekend?"

"Yes."

"Well, we stayed a little longer than we planned, or I would have called you sooner and then, when I did try to call, the lines were down, so just keep in mind that I *did* try to get hold of you and—"

"Will you just say it?" Keira demanded.

"He asked me to marry him," Kelly said, with a sigh that told Keira her little sister was no doubt staring at her engagement ring and getting all misty-eyed.

"He did?"

"Yes. I'm engaged."

"That's—" Keira didn't know what to say, so she said nothing at all. Her heart took a small ping of something she really didn't want to call envy, but there didn't seem to be any other name for it. Oh, God, Kelly was getting married. She was living in Europe and marrying a man who was crazy about her.

And Keira was standing still.

Not that she didn't like her life—she did.

But…she'd had so many plans once upon a time and none of them had come true. And now, despite being happy for her little sister, there was a small, whimpering voice in the back of her mind, wishing that things were different for her, too.

"I have the most beautiful ring you've ever seen, it's so amazing. We're getting married this summer. At his parents' estate in Sussex. Oh, Keira, it's going to be so gorgeous. So perfect. And Tony's so great. I really love him so much and everything is so wonderful."

No one but Kelly could cram that many *so's* into a single paragraph. Her palpable excitement hummed through the phone like a live electrical wire.

"That's great, honey," Keira said and she really meant it. She was glad for Kelly. Glad she'd found someone to love and to love her back. Glad that she was building a life she was happy with.

Really.

"So will you come?"

"To the wedding?" Keira asked, dumbfounded. "Of course I'll come to the wedding! I'm completely expecting to be in the wedding."

"You're my maid of honor, Keira," Kelly said, clearly

exasperated now. "But I'm not talking about you coming to the wedding. I want you to come see me now. Please, Keira. Come and see me. Get away for a while."

"This is about Nathan, isn't it?" Keira whispered, not wanting him to overhear her.

"Well, yeah," Kelly said. "I don't want you getting attached to somebody like him. I know you, Keira. And I'm afraid you're gonna set yourself up for another fall."

"Hey. Who's the big sister here? You or me?"

"What? Because I'm younger I can't be right?"

Keira glanced over her shoulder again to make sure Nathan was still in the great room where she'd left him, then she closed her eyes, took a deep breath and said, "Even if you're right, Kel, getting away wouldn't change anything."

"Oh, God," Kelly said with a sigh. "It really is too late, isn't it? I can hear it in your voice. You already love him."

Did she? Instantly, images of Nathan flashed through her mind. The day they met, that night at the town party, dancing with him under the stars, the panicked look in his eyes everytime someone in town tried to thank him for his donation.

Memories raced through her mind now, one after another, almost too fast to separate one from the other. She remembered his rarely seen smile and the stunned look on his features whenever she made him think beyond what he'd always done. The gleam in his eyes as his body moved within hers. The stillness of the coming storm as they took their walk around the lake.

Making love in front of the fire, shouting at him as he stood on the snow-covered deck, furious with her for locking him out. His carrying her up the stairs and catching her whenever she stumbled because she wasn't paying attention.

He was arrogant and abrasive and annoying.

And God help her, she was crazy about him.

Leaning her head against the icy glass again, she whispered, "Oh, Kelly. You're right. I *am* in love with him."

Ten

"No way this is happening," Keira whispered frantically. "I've known him only a couple of weeks."

"Uh-huh," Kelly muttered. "And just what is the time frame for falling in love? A month? Six?"

"This can't be happening." Keira thunked her head against the windowpane and welcomed the hard jolt. What an idiot she was. She'd been so busy spending time with Nathan so he wouldn't split, she hadn't noticed that she was falling in love with the man.

"Run," Kelly said. "Run fast, run far."

"I can't," Keira snapped. "Snowed in. Remember? Besides, it's too late for that."

Kelly sighed. "I know. What're you gonna do?"

"Well, I'm not telling him, that's for damn sure," she said. She might be an idiot, but she knew enough to know Nathan wouldn't want to hear her declaration of love any more than Max had.

No, thank you. She wasn't going to set herself up for another kick in the teeth. She'd made the mistake of falling in love with the wrong man. Again. But that didn't mean she had to let anyone else know.

"Probably a good plan," Kelly said, then added, "but if you want my advice…"

"I really don't."

"Well, that's nice."

"Kel, I'm sorry. But this one I'm going to have to take care of on my own."

"Fine. Just—watch yourself, okay?"

"Yeah." Keira inhaled sharply, blew the air out in a rush and said, "I've gotta go. I've got some thinking to do."

"Okay, but call me this weekend."

When she hung up, Keira didn't move. She just stood there, rooted in the kitchen, staring out at the storm and, for the first time in her life, she hated the snow. Hated the storm that was trapping her there with a man who didn't want her. Hated that she couldn't get away. Hated that she'd set herself up for more pain.

And mostly, she hated herself for being jealous of her little sister.

"Why is it that when Kelly falls in love, everything works out great?"

"Who you talking to?"

She spun around to see Nathan standing in the doorway, watching her. A flush of heat swept over her and she hoped to hell he hadn't overheard any of her conversation with Kelly. "No one. How long have you been there?"

"About ten seconds. Did you get hold of your sister?"

"Yes," Keira said, plastering a brilliant smile on her face. "She's terrific. Better than terrific, really. She's engaged."

"That's nice."

"Yeah," she said, shifting her gaze to the phone she still held in her hand, "it is."

"And you sound really excited for her."

"Oh, I am."

"Well, now I'm convinced," he said, walking over to the counter to pour himself another cup of coffee. "What's wrong, don't you like the guy?"

"Never met him, actually. Talked to him a couple of times, but they live in England, so…"

"Why don't you go visit?"

Keira looked up at him as he leaned casually against the kitchen counter, taking a sip of his coffee. "I believe we already covered that. I have responsibilities here."

One dark eyebrow rose. "So mayors don't get vacations?"

"Why do you care if I visit my sister or not?" she snapped.

"Whoa. Don't care. Just asked."

Keira held up one hand, crossed the room and gave him back his phone. "Sorry, sorry. That wasn't about you. That was about me."

He looked at her for a long minute or two and Keira stared up into those pale blue eyes of his. How could she not have realized that she was falling in love with him? And when had it happened?

When he told her about his awful grandmother? When he actually listened to her advice? When they took a walk beside the lake? When he touched her and made her body sing?

Oh, God.

Why couldn't she have fallen for the right guy this time?

"What's wrong?" he asked and his voice was so quiet, she nearly missed the words.

"I don't know," she said, because she couldn't tell him the truth. Turning her back on him, she walked to the windows and stared out at the storm that had become an enemy.

She heard his footsteps behind her, but didn't turn to watch him approach. Instead, she watched his reflection in the dark glass and, when his hands came down on her shoulders, she managed to suppress a sigh of satisfaction at his touch.

"Tell me," he said softly.

Keira shook her head and said, "I'm evil."

He laughed shortly. "Yeah? Evil how?"

"My sister tells me she's engaged and I'm envious. How evil is that?"

He dropped his hands from her shoulders and Keira thought he couldn't have made it any clearer just how he felt. He didn't move away, though. Just stood there behind her, his body sending waves of heat her way.

"You want to get married?"

Now *she* laughed a little. At the situation. At herself. At the raw panic in the reflection of his eyes.

"I always planned to," she said. "Just like I planned to travel. But things don't seem to work out the way you think they will."

"Maybe that's for the best."

She turned around to look up at him. "For the best?"

He shrugged. "Who cares what your old plans were? Thought you liked your life the way it is."

"I do," she admitted, "It's just…different from what I expected it to be. My mom used to say that life is what happens while you're making plans. And I guess that's true."

As she talked, Keira knew she was trying to convince not only Nathan, but herself, that her life was just the way she wanted it. That she would be fine when he left. That it didn't matter to her that he didn't love her. That he would be leaving without a backward glance.

She would be all right because she still had her home. Her place in the world. If it wasn't the place she'd always planned on, did that make it any less important? No.

"I mean," she said, pulling a chair out from under the kitchen table and plopping into it, "I love Hunter's Landing. I love belonging and being a part of the town's life. So, plan or no plan, I like my life. Don't get me wrong, I'd still like to travel, but this will always be home. I'll always come back here."

He looked down at her and shook his head, taking another sip of his coffee. "I don't understand tying yourself to a place."

Keira's heart felt another twinge, but she managed to avoid showing it. "The word *home* isn't synonymous with *prison*."

"Might as well be," he said. "The best way to live is to just keep moving."

Which is just what he'd be doing in a couple of weeks. He'd be moving on so fast that he probably wouldn't even bother to say goodbye. It hurt her to know that she'd remember him long after he'd forgotten her *and* Hunter's Landing. "Because if you keep moving, you make sure you never have time to care about anyone or anything, huh?"

His gaze narrowed on her. "You like sitting still. I like moving. Who's to say which way is best?"

"Me."

"Ah," he said, setting his coffee cup down onto the kitchen table. Shoving both hands into his pockets, he said irritably, "Ms. Roots speaks. Hearth and home and everything that goes with it, right? Well, not all of us are looking to get stuck in a rut so deep you can't see over the top of it."

"Who said anything about a rut?" she demanded, standing up so she was more on an even keel with him. It hadn't taken long for the two of them to start an argument. And maybe it was better this way, she thought. Maybe if they kept fighting, then it wouldn't hurt so much when he left.

But, even as she thought it, Keira knew it for a lie. She *liked* fighting with Nathan. So this would be just one more thing to miss.

"Please. Your rut is so comfortable, you've hung curtains and had it carpeted."

"Excuse me?"

"Come on, Keira. Admit it. You're stuck here in this little town, and the only reason you keep talking about how wonderful it is, is to keep yourself from feeling cheated out of the life you wanted."

"Is that right?" Incensed, she poked him in the chest with her index finger and seriously thought about kicking him. But she wasn't wearing shoes so she'd probably break her toe. "Just so you know, Mr. Fabulous World Traveler, I do *not* feel cheated. If I wanted my life to change, I'd change it. I'm not the one who's too afraid to try something new."

"Afraid?" He snorted a laugh. "Is that supposed to mean that *I'm* afraid of something?"

She blinked at him. "Duh."

"This should be good." He folded his arms over his chest, tipped his head to one side and waited, a smirking half smile on his face. "Fine. Tell me. What am I so afraid of?"

"I don't know," Keira admitted, wishing she did. Because then, maybe she'd have half a chance to fight through the walls he'd built around himself so many years ago.

"Hah!"

"But *you* know," she added quickly. "You might not admit it to me, but deep down inside, you know damn well there's a reason you're constantly moving on."

"Yeah," he said. "I like it."

"Liar."

He blew out a disgusted breath.

"You spend your whole life running so fast that nobody can catch up," Keira said, more thoughtful now as the temper that had spiked within her slowly drained away. "The question is what're you running from, Nathan?"

"I'm not running from anything."

"Well," she mused. "I guess you've said that often enough that even you believe it now."

She walked around him, careful not to brush against

him as she headed for the doorway leading back to the great room. When she reached it, she paused and looked back at him, standing alone in an elegant kitchen. This is how she'd remember him best, she thought. Stubbornly aloof. Alone.

Her heart ached, almost in preparation for the coming pain, but she held it inside as she said, "Someday, I hope you figure it out, Nathan. Before it's too late to stop and let somebody catch up to you."

She avoided him for the rest of the day and Nathan told himself he didn't care. He appreciated having some quiet time to work uninterrupted. God knew, since he'd met Keira, he'd had little enough peace and quiet.

And after an afternoon of it, he was going quietly insane.

He kept looking for her, expecting her to run into the room and trip over a table or something. He kept listening for the sound of her voice. But there was nothing. The big lodge fairly echoed with a stillness that was starting to really grate on him. Disgusted with himself, he finally realized that his satellite phone could connect him with more people than the citizens of Hunter's Landing.

Grabbing it, he hit the speed dial and called the one person on earth he knew would understand exactly what he was going through.

"Barton."

Nathan smiled at the sound of his old friend's voice. They hadn't really seen each other since college, but Luke Barton was one of the Seven Samurai he'd managed to keep in touch with, however loosely.

"Barrister here," he said and stalked to the wide

windows overlooking the white stillness covering the front yard of the lodge.

"Hell, Nathan." Luke laughed. "Good to hear your voice. How's life in the wild?"

"Not as wild as we might like," he grumbled and turned his back on the view of Mother Nature. "Glad to say my month is almost up and yours is coming."

"That bad?" Luke asked, dread clear in his voice.

"Small-town America at its coziest."

"Jeez. Sounds horrifying."

Nathan laughed and felt better. Good to know he wasn't the only person in the world who preferred big cities to quiet reflection. "Exactly. I got your e-mail last week," he said. "How the hell did Matthias convince you to switch months at the cabin with him? Are you two speaking again?"

"Not likely," Luke admitted.

The Barton twins had been at war for years, ever since their father had cooked up a competition between the two of them for the right to run the family business. Matthias won, but Luke was always sure his twin had somehow cheated him. Not that Luke was starving or anything. He'd built his own fortune—one to rival the legacy that Matthias had inherited—by starting up Eagle Wireless, a tech company that had pretty much taken over the world.

Still, old rivalries would never die.

"So, how'd Matt get you to switch?"

"Bastard couldn't do his month—some business emergency or other. Not sure, really. His assistant talked to my assistant." Luke blew out a disgusted breath. "The only reason I agreed to the damn switch was so Hunter's last request wouldn't be ruined."

Nathan wandered the great room while he listened. The house was crouched in quiet, and he was as cut off from the outside world as neatly as he would have been if he'd been on Mars. Talking to Luke took the edge off, and he wondered why the hell they didn't talk to each other more often.

"How bad is it?" Luke asked. "Have you at least been to Tahoe? Stateline?"

"No," Nathan answered. "I can see the lights from the casinos in the distance though—when it isn't snowing."

"Snowing?" Luke echoed. "It's March, for God's sake."

"And I'm talking to you from the middle of a blizzard."

"God, if Hunter wasn't gone, I'd kill him myself."

Nathan laughed again and dropped onto the couch. "Just what I was thinking when I first got here."

"But not now?"

"Don't get me wrong," Nathan said, "I can't wait to shake this place. Get the jet fired up and leave Hunter's Landing in the dust."

"But…"

"No but."

"I heard an implied but."

Frowning, Nathan said, "But there's a woman."

"Isn't there always? Who was that last one? Some Hollywood babe who wanted you to produce her next movie?"

He smiled, then frowned again. Maybe he was too used to people using him. "This one's different."

"This must be a sign of the Apocalypse," Luke said. "Nathan Barrister in love?"

"Who the hell said anything about love?" Nathan countered and jumped off the couch like he'd been set on fire.

"Okay then, I stand reassured," Luke said, then covered the receiver with one hand and muttered something Nathan couldn't catch. "Nathan," he said a moment later, "I've got to run. I have a meeting with some new Japanese clients and want to get this deal sewn up before I have to take my place in the cottage at the end of the world."

"Right. Well, hurry the hell up and get me out of this place, all right?"

"Not a chance, pal. You finish out your damn month. I've got my own to worry about."

After he'd hung up, Nathan stood in the middle of the great room and listened to the quiet. He should be glad Keira was giving him some space. It wasn't like he needed to be around her, for God's sake. But the quiet nagged at him and, when he finally couldn't stand it anymore, he went looking for her, sure that he'd find her sitting in a corner somewhere, pissed off and thinking of ways to make him suffer.

But she wasn't anywhere in the house.

Scowling, he grabbed his jacket from the hook in the mudroom, walked outside into the slap of an icy wind and squinted into the lamp-lit darkness. Even the night seemed deeper here. More black. More all-encompassing.

The moon was hidden behind clouds that showed no sign of leaving and snow was *still* falling, though in lighter flurries than before. He walked across the deck, grabbed the railing and leaned out, scanning the area for her.

"Surely she wouldn't have gone on one of her *walks* in the snow," he muttered. And as he considered that, he imagined her lying on the ground, unconscious from hitting her head when she fell because *he* hadn't been there to catch her. She could freeze to death out there and no one would find her until the spring thaw—if spring ever really came to the high Sierras.

Ridiculous. He tried to dismiss the worry. She'd managed to survive without his help for thirty years; he was sure she'd be fine tonight, too. "But she could have told me where she was going," he said softly.

An explosion of icy wet hit the side of his head and Nathan jerked upright like he'd been shot. Almost before he realized that he'd been hit with a snowball, he heard her laugh and turned toward the sound.

Keira stood beneath the deck, her breath puffing out in white clouds in front of her. Her smile stretched across her face and her laughter rose up in the air like music.

"Got ya!"

"Are you out of your mind?" he shouted to be heard over her wild whoop of renewed amusement.

"What's the matter, Nathan?" she taunted. "Afraid of a little snow?" Then she bent down, scooped up more of the icy stuff, patted it into a ball and let it go.

This time he saw it coming and ducked. And while he was bent down low, he scooped up some snow of his own, packed a mean snowball and let it fly while she was bent over gathering new ammunition. He hit her on the back of the head and she went down on one knee.

Instantly, he worried that he'd actually hurt her. A second later though, she raised her gaze to his and said, "You realize this means war."

He'd never get used to her, he thought. While he had been expecting to find her sulking and nursing a temper—as most other women he'd ever known would have been doing—she had been outside waiting for the opportunity to execute a surprise attack.

She wasn't angry. She was laughing. And the joy in that sound touched something inside Nathan that had been locked away for more years than he could count. He didn't examine it too closely. Instead, he gave himself up to the moment. He forgot about work. Forgot about keeping a safe distance from a woman who too easily found her way around his defenses. He forgot everything in the moment that was *now.*

"You're gonna pay for this," he shouted.

"Talk is cheap," she taunted.

Setting one hand on the railing, he vaulted over the edge and landed five feet down in the snow, bending his knees to absorb the jolt.

Her eyes went wide, and stunned surprise kept her frozen just long enough to give Nathan time to form another snowball and let her have it. She shrieked when the snow hit her face and did a funny little dance as some of the cold wet stuff slinked beneath the collar of her jacket.

But she didn't let it slow her down. In seconds the war was raging and the two of them were running around the snowy yard like a couple of ten-year-olds. Nathan hadn't had so much fun in years. He couldn't remember the last time he'd done anything like this and he was loving it. Their shouts echoed off the mountain and snow flew from half-frozen hands like white bullets.

Lamplight gleamed golden and shone in her hair as Nathan circled her, waiting for an opening. When he got it, he charged her, grabbing her around the waist and carrying them both to the snowy cushion atop the cold ground. He hit the ground first, taking the brunt of the fall, keeping her on top of him until he rolled over her, pinning her in place.

"I win," he said, grinning at her.

"No fair," she countered. "I didn't know we were playing tackle snow war."

"All's fair," he said—then caught himself before he could utter the rest of the old cliché.

She smiled up at him and the warmth in her gaze started a fire inside him that burned away every icy edge he had ever carried. He felt…different somehow and, later, when he thought about this moment, he might do some worrying. But right now, all he wanted to think about was her. What she did to him with a smile. How she could constantly surprise him and jolt him out of the ordinary.

And just how much he wanted her.

Bending his head to hers, he kissed her and the cold of her lips met his, eagerly, hungrily. When he finally broke free, he said, "How about we finish this inside?"

Eleven

Two days later, the lodge phone rang and Keira nearly jumped out of her skin. Nathan grabbed it and, after a second or two, handed it over to her. A brief conversation later, she hung up, looked at Nathan and said, "Phone lines are working again."

His mouth quirked and she felt a tug in the pit of her stomach. Something like the beginnings of loneliness. Their time together was over and it was time to go back to the real world. The world where Nathan wasn't a part of her life.

"I got that. How about the roads?" he asked.

Keira raised her chin and gave him a bright smile. "Your prayers are answered. That was Bill Hambleton, the deputy mayor. He was calling to let me know the crews were out and the road to the lodge should be clear by late afternoon."

"Bill, huh?" Nathan nodded, picked up the remote and turned the TV off in the middle of the movie they had been watching. "How'd he know you were here?"

"His wife, Patti, knew I was coming here the day the storm hit." She shrugged. "Guess she just figured when she didn't see me in town that I had gotten stuck here."

"His wife," he mused.

"Yeah." Keira cocked her head and smiled at his expression. Was it possible he had been—even momentarily—jealous?

"So you'll be leaving."

"Time to go home."

"For some of us."

"You're the one who said you didn't have a home," she reminded him.

"Touché," he acknowledged with a nod. "I guess I meant that one of us will be leaving."

"So, you'll definitely stay for the rest of the month?"

Nodding, he leaned back into the couch. "Yeah. I'll stay."

"Thanks," she whispered and resisted the urge to reach out and smooth his hair back from his forehead.

"It's okay." He propped his feet up on the coffee table and said, "It's only two weeks. And, hell," he added quietly, more to himself than to her, "guess I owe it to Hunter."

Keira leaned into the couch too, curling her legs up under her. "Tell me about him."

"What?"

"Hunter Palmer," she urged. "Tell me about him. I mean, all I know is that, for some reason, he chose our town to build his lodge in—and he's arranged for some amazingly generous donations to charity."

Nathan looked at her briefly, then shifted his gaze so that he was staring at the fire burning in the hearth. As if mesmerized by the flames, he began talking slowly, as if unsure just where to start. "My guess is Hunter chose your town because its name was the same as his. Probably thought it was a good joke. Anyway, we went to college together. Hunter, me, and the other guys who'll be coming here."

"Where?"

"Harvard," he said easily, and she wondered if he knew he was smiling. "After our first year, we rented a house off campus together."

"Just you and Hunter?"

"No, all seven of us. Back then we called ourselves the Seven Samurai." He shot her an amused look. "Not real clever, but…" He shrugged and let it go. "We were all as close as brothers back then."

"I was looking at the framed photos of all of you in the upstairs hall yesterday," Keira said. "Your hair was a lot longer then."

He chuckled at that, and she thought he looked a little surprised. "Don't remind me."

"Oh, I don't know. I sort of like a man in a ponytail."

His smile slowly faded as he shook his head. Firelight shimmered in the room, and Keira watched as memories swarmed in the depths of his eyes. "We were different then. All of us," he said, his voice soft and far away. "We were so certain how life would turn out for us. That night we promised to build this lodge together, it never crossed our minds that we wouldn't all be there to see it." He paused. "Hunter got sick our senior year. Skin cancer. By the time they found it, it was way too late. He died by inches."

"Oh, Nathan."

He let his head fall to the back of the sofa and stared up at the ceiling. "I watched him sliding away and finally one night I couldn't take it anymore. I went to a bar near the campus, got blind drunk and picked a fight." A quirk of his mouth appeared and disappeared again a moment later. "Naturally, I picked the wrong guy to mess with and got my ass kicked. I ended up in the hospital."

Keira's heart ached listening to him, but she knew she had to let him finish. She had the distinct impression that he'd never said any of this before.

He turned his head to look at her. "I woke up three days later and found out Hunter had died and was already buried."

"I'm sorry."

A closed door snapped into place over his eyes and his voice lost the memory-tinged softness. "It was a long time ago."

"It was yesterday."

He turned and speared her with a look. "What's that supposed to mean?"

"Nathan, I can see it in your face," she said gently. "The pain of it is still with you."

"You're wrong," he said and pushed himself to his feet. Shoving his hands into his pockets, he walked around the room like a caged tiger looking for a way through the bars. "It was ten years ago, Keira. I'm over it."

"I wish that was true," she said softly. "But it's not." Shaking her head, she got up from the couch, crossed the room and stopped right in front of him. Reaching up, she cupped his face between her palms. "Whether you can admit it or not, you're punishing yourself for a single mistake you made when you were in pain. Don't you see that Hunter wouldn't want you to be so alone? Still suffering over something you never meant to do?"

"Oh, for God's sake," he said, pulling away from her touch, "I'm not a wounded animal, Keira. Or a child. I don't want or need your sympathy."

"Well, you have it anyway," she said.

Shaking his head, he choked out a strangled laugh. "God. I don't know how you got me talking about this, but don't think I'm looking to be *cured*. I'm not carrying around a burden of guilt for being a stupid kid. I'm not hiding myself away from people so that I never have to worry about letting someone down when they need me again."

"I didn't say that's why you're alone so much," she pointed out quietly, "but it's interesting that it's the first thing that came to you."

"This is great," he snapped, pushing one hand through his hair and looking like he'd rather be anywhere but where he was at the moment. "A mayor who's a part-time psychiatrist. Lucky for me you were here."

"Nathan…"

"Forget it, Keira. I'm not interested in being analyzed."

"I wasn't—"

"Yes, you were. Well, don't bother. I'm not 'punishing' myself," he said, his voice as grim as the bleak shine in his eyes. "I'm just living."

"Are you?" she asked. "Really?"

He laughed sourly and shook his head. "You're seeing things that aren't there, Keira. Quit fooling yourself. I'm not the man you think I am," he said. "I'm not looking to be saved. I'm not looking for roots. My life is just the way I want it. I'm happy going from Monte Carlo to Venice to London. I have friends, I go to parties, I come and go as I please and I live exactly the way I want to live. Not all of us want to be buried alive in a small town on top of a mountain."

Her heart twisted in her chest as she looked up at him and watched him emotionally pull further away from her than he'd ever been. "Nathan…"

He took a long step backward. "Just leave it alone, okay? Today you go back to your life. I go back to mine. And it's probably best if we just don't see each other again while I'm here."

There it was—the pain she'd been waiting for since the moment she realized she was in love with him. God. She hadn't expected it to be so sharp. So devastating. When Max had betrayed her, she'd thought herself wounded. But now, knowing that she was losing Nathan, Keira finally understood what real misery was. What real heartbreak was.

Instantly, her imagination played out in her mind, showing her the coming years. The long, lonely years when she would be wondering if he ever thought of her. If he missed her. If he ever wished he had stayed in Hunter's Landing.

And in the next moment, Keira had to ask herself if she would come to regret never telling him that she loved him. If she didn't, she'd never know if there might have been a chance for them. Besides, if she kept quiet about her feelings, hiding behind her fear, wouldn't that make her as big a coward as Nathan—hiding from possible pain?

That thought was enough to spur her into action. She

would take a chance because that's who she was. Who she had always been. And if he didn't want her, then she would know. If he didn't love her, she'd never have to wonder. She would only have to mourn what might have been.

"Maybe you're right," she said after taking a moment to steady herself. "Maybe we shouldn't see each other anymore. But before I leave, I want you to know something."

His jaw clenched and his pale blue eyes shone with wariness. "I really think we've said enough already."

"I don't," she countered quickly, before she could talk herself out of this. "You may not want to hear this, but I'm going to say it because if I don't, I know I'll regret it and, damn it, there are enough regrets in the world already."

"Keira…"

"I love you," she said, the words dropping into a sudden silence like stones into a well. When he didn't say anything, Keira pushed on, knowing that if she didn't get it all said now, she might never have another chance. "I didn't expect to, but I do. I really love you, Nathan."

Suspicion glittered in his eyes now, and she knew she was fighting in a battle already lost. He'd closed himself off so tightly, she could barely see a shadow of the man she'd spent the last four days with. But still, she'd come this far; she would say the rest, too.

"I'm not expecting you to say anything, and hey," she forced a short laugh she didn't feel "good thing. And I don't want anything from you, either. I just…wanted you to know that somebody loves you. That *I* love you."

She couldn't reach him. She could see it as plain as anything. He had withdrawn so far from her, it was as if she was alone in the room.

The silence screamed at her. The snap and hiss of the fire sounded as loud as gunshots. While she watched him, Keira remembered everything they'd shared here during the storm. The wild, passionate lovemaking, the snowball fight, the arguments and the laughter.

She recalled turning to him in the middle of the night and feeling his arms slide around her middle, pinning her to him as they slept, and she wondered how she would ever sleep through the night again without him. How was she going to face every day, knowing she wouldn't see him? Would never talk to him again?

A soul-deep ache washed over her and Keira wanted to moan at the swell of looming emptiness inside. But she didn't. If this was the last time she was going to see him, then she wanted him to remember her smiling. And maybe someday, when it was much too late for either of them, he would think back to this moment and wish he'd had the courage to accept the love she had offered him.

"Well," she said briskly, giving him her brightest smile and hoping it was enough to ease the shadows she knew were in her eyes, "I guess that's it. The road should be clear in a couple of hours, so I'll just stay out of your hair until then."

He nodded so stiffly, it was a wonder his neck didn't snap.

Keira walked up to him, went up on her toes and planted a quick, fierce kiss on his unyielding mouth. Then she stepped back, looked into his eyes and whispered, "Goodbye, Nathan Barrister."

Then she left him, and the only sounds in the room were the fire and her quick steps as she ran up the staircase to get her things.

* * *

Several hours later, Keira was gone and the big house on the lake echoed with emptiness. Nathan wandered from room to room, too restless to sit still, too wired to work. Instead, his mind continued to taunt him by replaying those last few moments with Keira.

She loved him.

He should have said something, but damned if he knew what. She'd caught him completely off balance and that wasn't something that happened to Nathan Barrister. He was a man who always knew where he stood. What to do. What to expect. He'd made a habit of being prepared for any eventuality.

She loved him.

He took the stairs two steps at a time, listening to the sound of his own footsteps thump like a jittering heartbeat in the big house. When he hit the upper landing, he headed for the bedroom. But, instead of averting his gaze from the old photos on the wall, he stopped to look at them all for the first time.

Echoes of the past reached out for him as his gaze moved from one familiar face to the next. There was Hunter, of course, laughing into the camera without a care in the world. And Nathan smiled at the photo of Luke and Matt Barton, back in the days when they were still speaking, holding Ryan Sperling in a friendly headlock, while Devlin Campbell and Jack Howington poured bottles of beer over them all.

His friends. More than friends, they'd been brothers—the only real family Nathan had known after his parents' death. And he'd let them all slip mostly away from him.

When Hunter died, the rest of the group had splintered, as if its heart had been removed and there was no way to keep the rest of the whole together. Nathan reached out and touched the glass covering a photo of the Seven Samurai and he realized just how much he missed them all. How he missed what they had been back then!

And he wondered what kind of man he might have been if things had been different.

Would he have known how to accept Keira's love? Would he have believed her when she said she wanted nothing from him? Shaking his head, he stepped back from the images of his past and walked on, into the master bedroom.

No. How could he believe her? *Everyone* wanted something from him, he thought as he laid down, fully clothed across the bed. Why should she be any different?

One day bled into the next and that one into another until a week had crawled past.

And Nathan hadn't gotten a damn thing done.

No lists. No memos. No e-mails to hotel managers setting up meetings. Instead, he was restless. Couldn't think. Couldn't sleep. Couldn't keep his mind from turning to thoughts of Keira, damn it.

She was everywhere in the lodge. He couldn't take a step without remembering something she had said. He couldn't lay in bed without recalling the feel of her body pressed to his. He couldn't walk into the kitchen without seeing her naked on the counter. He stepped outside and was whisked back to the night of their snowball fight. He went for firewood and remembered her locking him outside and shouting at him through the glass.

He walked down the stairs and remembered catching her as she fell—and, damn it, he was worried about who was going to catch her when he wasn't around.

"Not my problem," he grumbled into the silence. "If the damn woman is too busy to watch where she's going, she'll just have to fall. Probably break her damn neck one of these days."

The quiet mocked him as his own voice faded into the stillness crouched in the big, empty lodge. One week to go and then he could leave. He had to stick it out now; he'd promised Keira, and a Barrister never went back on his word. No matter the temptation.

Scowling, he told himself that Keira was probably worried that he was going to leave anyway. Probably hadn't believed him when he'd promised. Well, he could just go into town and assure her that he would be right where he said he would be. That he was staying until the end of the month and then he was going to leave this town and *her* behind him as fast as he was able.

But, even as he thought that, something else occurred to him. Something he hadn't considered before and, frankly, at the moment, he couldn't figure out why not. It made sense. It fit the situation and would give both he and Keira what they wanted.

Damned if he wasn't a genius.

A week with no word from Nathan, and Keira was forced to admit that he just wasn't interested in what she felt for him. Of course, she hadn't really expected him to do an about-face, shout *I love you, too!* and carry her off to his castle—er, favorite hotel.

"But damn it, he doesn't have to completely ignore

me, either." She kicked her living room couch and limped into the kitchen for yet another cup of coffee. "It's my own fault," she muttered before taking a sip. "I knew who he was and how he felt, and I went ahead and fell in love with him anyway."

If she could have figured out exactly how to do it, she would have kicked her own ass.

"Idiot." She cupped both hands around her coffee mug and hoped that the heat would wipe away the chill sweeping through her. But it didn't help. Nothing would and she knew it. She was going to carry this icy loneliness around with her for the rest of her life. All because of one stubborn, miserable, selfish son of a bitch who didn't have the decency to accept an offer of love freely given.

"There. That's better," she whispered. "Be mad, not sad."

But the sad went too deep and the mad wasn't nearly enough to bury it.

When the doorbell rang, she set her coffee down and went to answer it. With any luck, there was some town crisis she could lose herself in. She threw the door open and stared up at Nathan, way too shocked to think of anything to say.

He smiled, and Keira swallowed hard. "What're you doing here?"

Stepping past her, he walked into her house, looked around, then turned to look at her, a wide smile brightening his features. "I have a surprise for you."

Intrigued and, damn it all, a little hopeful, Keira closed the door, shoved her hands into her jeans pockets and said, "A surprise?"

"Yes." He looked so pleased with himself, Keira

didn't know what to think. "I took care of everything this morning. You don't have to do a thing."

Worry began to nibble at her. He was taking care of everything? Taking care of what, exactly? "What is this great surprise then?"

He walked toward her, took hold of her shoulders and held on as he looked down into her eyes. "You know I'm leaving for Barbados at the end of the month."

"Yeah…" That sinking sensation in the pit of her stomach simply refused to go away.

"You're going with me."

Keira staggered and probably would have fallen down if his grip on her shoulders hadn't tightened perceptibly. "I'm what?"

He grinned, apparently taking her shock for pleasure. "I talked to your deputy mayor—Hambleton?"

"Bill, yes." She was struggling for air. Her chest felt tight and her whole body was tingling with nerves that were pushing her to do *something*.

"Right," he said. He released her, then walked into the living room and spun around, folding his arms across his chest, looking like a king who had finally figured out how to please the peasants. "I told Bill you'd be leaving with me and we didn't know how long we'd be gone. He's fine with it. He can handle whatever happens here—" He shrugged. "Town this size, running it can't be too difficult anyway."

"Is that right?" Cold. She felt cold all the way through. How weird. For the last week, she'd alternated between fury and grief, and now all she could feel was this body-numbing iciness.

"I called the hotel in Barbados," he was saying. "Told

them I would have a companion accompanying me and arranged for a personal shopper for you the moment we land. You don't even have to pack for the trip. While I'm working, you'll have the run of the shops—unlimited expense account, of course—and we'll have every night to ourselves."

"I see." She really did and she was hurt in more ways than she could count.

"From Barbados," he said, hurrying on to fill the silence growing between them, "we'll head to London. Maybe visit your sister. Or even better, we'll go to Venice—I'll send for your sister, make all the arrangements. You can have her with you as long as you want."

"How nice for me—you can arrange Kelly's life, too."

He frowned briefly, shoved one hand through his hair and said, "If you don't want to go to Venice, we'll go somewhere else."

"Oh," Keira said, walking past him now, into the kitchen where she picked up her coffee cup. "I get a vote?"

"What?"

She took a breath, hoping to steady the swell of fury rising up to choke her. "And if I tell you I can't afford to take off work? To go and travel around the world with you?"

"I didn't ask you to pay for anything," he said, frowning. "I've taken care of it. I told you that."

"Right. Silly me. So *you* decide what I do and where I go. *You* pay for me and I'm supposed to just be grateful to be taken care of."

"Is there something wrong with that?"

He was looking at her like she was speaking Greek. Could he really be this clueless?

"You really don't see it, do you?" Keira felt like her head was exploding. How could she ever make him see who she really was if he was convinced his bank account would fix any problem?

"I'm offering you the travel and excitement you always dreamed of and that makes me a bad guy?"

"You didn't even *ask* me, Nathan. You just order me here or there, and I'm supposed to come trotting along behind you fluttering with gratitude?"

"I'm confused," he admitted and stopped in the doorway between the kitchen and the living room. "You said you wanted to travel."

"Yeah, I did."

"You want to visit your sister. See Venice."

"All correct," she admitted, and took a sip of coffee that she didn't even taste. Heck, she was half amazed that she could force the liquid down past the knot in her throat.

"Then what's the problem? Why the hell aren't you happy?" He was shouting now, and that at least made her feel a little better. She'd finally cracked through his wall of blasé.

"Because you *told* me what I was going to do," she countered, slapping her cup down onto the counter with enough force to slosh coffee over the edge. "You didn't ask. You just arranged everything the way you wanted it to be. God, you went to Bill and told him we'd be traveling together. That's just fabulous."

"You said you loved me," he said tightly. "I naturally assumed you would want to be with me."

Keira choked out a laugh. "And because I love you I would want to be your 'companion'? How many times have your hotel employees been told to prepare for your current 'guest'? What number am I in line? Is there a salary that goes with the position? How much does your own private whore make? Am I paid by the hour? Or is my new wardrobe my payment?"

"For God's sake, that's not how I meant—"

"You're unbelievable," Keira said, striding across the kitchen to slap both hands against his chest. "You go behind my back to *arrange* my life. Oh, and you don't even stop there. You think you can arrange my *sister's* life—she has a job, you know? And a fiancé. She can't just entertain me when it's convenient for you."

"This is not the way I expected this conversation to go," he said.

"Well, maybe you should have written out a script for me."

"Damn it, that's not what I meant. I thought you'd be happy. I thought you wanted to travel. To see the world. That's what you said."

"I said a lot of things. Some of them you obviously ignored. I *love* my home. I don't want to leave it forever, and I can't just walk away from my responsibilities here because you say so."

He inhaled sharply, deeply, and blew the air out in a long rush of exasperation. Well, now she knew just how he felt. She loved the man and now she knew all too well that he would never love her back.

"I didn't tell you I loved you so that you would *do* something for me, Nathan," she said, and all of her anger drained away in the wash of despair swamping her. "My love doesn't come with a price tag. You don't have to throw presents at me to try to even the playing field. I didn't ask for anything from you. I offered you my love, free and clear. No strings attached."

"Keira—"

"You know what? I think you should go, Nathan," she said, moving past him to the front door, locking her knees so that she wouldn't slump to the floor until long after he left. "You just don't understand me and you never will."

He stopped beside her and looked down into her eyes for one brief moment. "You're right," he said. "I don't understand you. I offered you everything you ever wanted and you turned it all down."

"Not everything, Nathan," she said, and quietly closed the door behind him.

Twelve

Keira smiled and tried to focus on her friend standing in front of her. It wasn't easy. For a week now she'd been moving in a fog. She couldn't get Nathan out of her mind and she wondered if she'd spend the rest of her life like this—only half aware of the world going on around her.

She'd had to tell several people that she wasn't actually leaving with Nathan at the end of the month. And she'd had to put up with their knowing smiles and nods of sympathy for a love affair gone bad. Damn Nathan anyway. By trying to run her life, he'd made it that much more complicated.

"The contractor says he's ready to start on the clinic next week," Mike McDonald was saying, and Keira made an effort to concentrate.

"He wants to start before the thaw?"

Mike, an older man with long gray hair that he kept in a neat ponytail, shrugged and said, "He says he wants to start on the inside and then, by the time the snows are gone, his crew will be ready to begin the structural changes."

"Okay," she said, nodding as she shifted her gaze to the clinic that was going to become so much more, thanks to Nathan's contribution and the promise of Hunter Palmer's legacy. "I'll tell the town council and you can give the contractor the go ahead."

"Great," Mike said, adding, "and you're gonna be here, right?"

She sighed. "Yes, Mike. I'll be here. I live here. Where else would I be?"

He clucked his tongue and patted her shoulder before heading off down the sidewalk.

Alone, Keira turned and took in all of Hunter's Landing in a single glance. A sad smile curved her mouth as she realized what an idiot she had been to think that a man like Nathan would want to give up his travels to exotic cities and countries in favor of settling down in a tiny town like this one.

Kelly had been right. Nathan was *so* not the right man for Keira. He'd proven that himself only two days ago when he'd tried to hijack her life. "Unfortunately," she whispered, her heart as heavy as it had been the last time she'd seen him, "he's the only one I want."

"Talking to yourself, Mayor?" Francine Hogan called from the doorway of the post office.

Jolted, Keira forced a smile. "Nobody understands me better than me," she joked.

Just as Keira had hoped, Francine laughed and went

about her business. Stuffing her hands into her pockets, Keira walked down the street, nodding and smiling at the people she'd known her whole life.

The sun was shining and the temperature was finally starting to climb. Maybe spring was actually going to arrive at last. Just in time for Nathan to shake off the dust of Hunter's Landing and move on to Barbados. Without her. She felt a twinge around her heart and knew that it was something she was just going to have to get used to.

Then she stopped and blinked. Okay, she was worse off than she'd thought. If she didn't know better, she would swear that Nathan Barrister was standing outside the grocery store, chatting with Sallye Carberry. Oh, Keira thought, she was really losing it.

Putting one hand up to shield her eyes, she took a better look and could hardly believe what she was seeing. It *was* Nathan. Smiling and talking as if he and the older woman were the best of friends. As she stood, rooted to the spot, she watched him say goodbye to Sallye, then move along the walk on the opposite side of the street, stopping now and then to greet someone else he'd met at the block party three weeks before. For a man so determined to be alone, he had already made connections with some of these people, whether he realized it or not.

"What is he doing?" she murmured, then followed that up with, "and why do I care?"

It was no business of hers what Nathan did. He had promised to stay in town through the end of the month and that was all that mattered now. And, since their last fight two days ago, she knew that any chance they might have had together was gone. Still, her heartbeat quickened and her mouth went dry just watching him walk. Oh, she really didn't want him to see her.

So, to minimize the risk of that happening, Keira hurried her steps, heading to the diner. She needed coffee and some comfort food, and the diner was the best place to find both.

Several days later, Nathan sat, having a solitary drink on the Clearwater restaurant's deck. He'd been in town every day now for nearly a week and he hadn't seen Keira once. Everywhere he went, people told him he'd just missed her. How was that possible in a town this size? Was she deliberately avoiding him? All because he'd wanted her with him? What in the hell did the woman want, anyway?

He stared out over the lake and watched the first deep, rich colors of sunset stain the sky. Around him, families laughed and talked together; waiters moved through the crowd with expert agility and, directly across from Nathan, a young couple sat so lost in each other they might as well have been alone on a deserted island.

A ping of envy rattled Nathan enough that he took a long drink of his Scotch and shifted his gaze back to the lake. Rose and gold streaks lay across the surface of the water and the cool evening breeze was so different from the icy wind that had held the mountain in a tight grip just the week before, it amazed him.

"Your usual, Mr. Barrister?" The waiter was standing beside his table, smiling.

"Yes, Jake. Thanks." As the young man moved off to get his dinner, Nathan surprised himself by smiling. He had, over the last few days, become a regular at the

Clearwater. The waiters knew his name and his favorite meal—the chicken Alfredo, no surprise there—and always greeted him like family.

But then, he'd been experiencing the same feelings all over town. The shop owners smiled, people stopped to talk with him and he had begun to feel as if he actually *belonged* in Hunter's Landing. A strange feeling for a man who had spent most of his life on the move. Even stranger…he liked it.

In a couple of days, his month would be over and he would be leaving. And the truth of it was, he'd never been less interested in moving on—alone. But Keira wouldn't come with him and he didn't know *how* to stay. Didn't know how to become a part of something greater than himself.

Didn't know how to love someone like Keira—and the thought of somehow screwing up what they had so briefly had together…making her sorry she'd ever said she loved him, was enough to make him see that leaving was really his only option.

He finished his drink and ordered another.

An hour later, Keira took her sandwich into the living room, dropped onto the couch and flipped on the television. She used to love sitting in the quiet, letting her mind rest after listening to people chatter all day long. But these days, she needed the noise. The distraction.

Because, in the quiet, her brain was too free to wander—and inevitably, it went straight to thoughts of Nathan. She took a bite of her grilled cheese sandwich, blindly stared at the game show playing out on the screen and thought about how Nathan had looked that afternoon.

She'd hidden inside the diner and watched him laughing with Bill Hambleton. The man who had fought so hard against staying in Hunter's Landing now seemed perfectly at home here. She'd been ducking him for days, not wanting to get close enough to be hurt again, but somehow needing to see him while she could.

"Pitiful. A thirty-year-old sixth grader," she muttered, setting her sandwich down on the coffee table. "That's what you are now, Keira. Aren't you proud?"

She flopped back into the couch cushions and pulled a pillow onto her chest. Wrapping her arms around it tightly, she hugged it to her, stared at the blasted TV and tried to concentrate on the inane game show host who was trying to be funny.

But how could she focus on anything but the fact that Nathan would be leaving in a few days? She thought about calling him now, telling him she'd changed her mind and would go with him, but she couldn't. She couldn't let him think that what she felt for him was temporary. Or that she was just another woman in a long line of impermanent lovers. But how could she let him go without talking to him again? And how could she face him without wanting to kiss him? Or kick him?

"God. I'm an idiot."

A knock on the door sounded out and she rolled to her feet, reluctantly pulling herself up and out of her own misery. As much as she wanted a distraction from her own thoughts, she was in no mood for company. She walked across the room, pulled the door open and said, "Nathan?"

He looked so good, it made her heart hurt. Why was he here?

"Keira," he said, shoving one hand through his hair, as his heated gaze raked her up and down. "I had to see you."

Hope leaped up into her chest and nearly strangled her. Was he here to admit that he cared? To tell her he wanted her as much as she wanted him? Her mouth went dry and her stomach did a weird pitch-and-roll that made her reach out and slap one hand to the doorjamb to keep herself upright. "What is it?"

He stepped past her into the house, not waiting for an invitation. When she closed the door and turned around to look at him, he was looking around her house. "I didn't say anything the other day, but this is a nice place."

"Thanks," she said, glancing at him over her shoulder as she moved past him into the living room. "Smaller than the lodge, but I like it."

Her knee caught the edge of a chair and Nathan reached out to steady her. His hand on her elbow sent bolts of heat rocketing through her body like frenzied lightning strikes in the middle of a summer storm. God, she'd missed that sensation.

"Still tripping, I see," he whispered, then let her go.

In a few days, there'd be no one around to catch her when she stumbled. She'd have dozens of small aches and bruises competing with the giant ache in her heart. She rubbed her elbow as if she could ease away the hum he'd created, and looked up at him. "Why are you here, Nathan?"

"I'm sorry we ended things the way we did," he said tightly.

"But not sorry we ended," she whispered, feeling a quick stab of fresh pain. So he wasn't here to grovel and beg her to take him back. When would she stop being an idiot?

He scrubbed one hand over his face, then reached into his jacket pocket. "I wanted to see you in person again. To give you this."

He handed her a folded slip of paper. Keira knew what it was before she opened it. Hadn't he given her one before? A personal check. Made out to Hunter's Landing. Only this check was for *one million dollars*.

"I want the town to have that," he was saying, and she could barely hear him over the roaring in her ears. "The clinic can become a first-class hospital and I want—"

"What?" Keira ground the word out as she tore her eyes from the check to meet his gaze. "You want what exactly? To be a hero? To be remembered? Well, the money isn't necessary, Nathan. I'll remember you just fine without it."

"Keira…"

"No," she snapped, fury rising up to swamp her pain, "you already made a huge donation, and I don't need you to throw more money at me because you're feeling guilty."

"Guilty?" he repeated.

"You're unbelievable," Keira said, riding that anger gratefully, because rage was so much easier to handle than pain. "I offered you *love* and you offer to make me your mistress. And when I turn that lovely offer down, you offer me cash."

"Damn it, Keira, this is all I *can* do. All I know how to do."

"Bull," she said and angrily swiped at the one stray tear that coursed down her cheek as she faced him down. "I can see in your eyes that you want to stay. I've watched you with everyone these last few days. I've seen you in town and you *like* it here, Nathan. I know that you want to be more, have more in your life. But you're too scared to try. Too caught up in your own careful world to take a risk—even if it means cheating yourself out of a real life."

He stalked away from her, whirled around to face her again and said, "I offered to take you with me."

"As your 'companion.'"

"I wanted you with me, I don't care what you call it," he said. "I never promised you anything, Keira. I made it clear right from the first that I wasn't the kind of man you needed."

"How the hell do you know what kind of man I need?" she argued. "Nathan, look at you. You've completely forgotten how to give *yourself* because giving money is so much easier. You hand out checks so you don't have to get involved. It lets you stay in the shadows, safe at a distance."

He didn't say anything though she waited a moment or two, desperately hoping he'd argue with her, tell her she was wrong and he *did* want a life. With her. When the words didn't come, Keira shook her head, crumpled his check in one tight fist and then shoved it into his jacket pocket.

"You already donated money for the clinic," she said, pride coloring her tone now as much as fury. "And the town will get its share of Hunter Palmer's bequest when the six months is up. We don't need more from you."

"Keira—"

"Go away, Nathan," she said, sorrow filling her voice and staining the words until she was sure she could see the pain she was feeling actually coloring the air. "Just leave. Go back to your travels. Go to Barbados. Find some woman who'll want your money so you'll know what to do with her. Move from hotel to hotel, making sure to never speak to anyone. Keep your insulated life because I don't want you *or* your money."

Nathan couldn't breathe. He looked into her stormy green eyes, heard her order him out of her house and knew that if he left, he was a dead man. He'd come here telling himself he only wanted to give her money for the town she loved. Telling himself he only wanted to see her one last time.

When she'd turned down his offer to travel with him, he'd been lost. He had been so sure she'd accept. He'd never had anyone turn him down before. Never had anyone tell him that what he could buy for them wasn't enough. He'd been so damned sure that she'd throw her own life away to follow him. And he hadn't even admitted to himself how important it had been that she come with him. He hadn't wanted to see just how much she meant to him.

When she told him to leave, he'd felt more alone than he ever had before. He couldn't see the coming years without Keira in them. He couldn't see himself without her in his life.

She was right. He was a damn liar.

Panic clawing at him, he reached out, grabbed hold of her and yanked her up against him. Wrapping his arms tight around her waist, he bent his head to the curve of her neck and inhaled her scent, drawing his first easy breath since the day she'd walked out of the lodge and out of his life.

"Keira, don't," he whispered, his words muffled against her skin. "Don't ask me to leave again. I'll do anything in the world for you but that."

She pulled her head back to look up at him, and it tore at him to see tears swimming in those brilliant green depths. This is what he'd brought her to. He'd reduced an incredibly strong woman to tears. He felt like the biggest jackass in the world.

"Nathan, I can't do this anymore," she said, shaking her head and squirming in his arms, trying to get free.

"Keira," he said quickly, holding her as if his life depended on it—because it did. "Don't cry," he said, bending his head to kiss away her tears before saying, "I'm so sorry. I tried to tell myself I could go back to my old life. Tried to believe it. Tried to convince myself that nothing had changed and that my life could continue along as usual. Hell, I tried to drag you into my old life, thinking that having you temporarily would ease the need I feel for you."

"Nathan—"

He moved his hands to cup her face, to stroke the pads of his thumbs across her cheeks. "But the truth is, nothing is the same for me anymore, Keira. You changed everything. I *love* you."

She sucked in a gulp of air and hope lit her eyes. Nathan smiled, finally feeling hope himself. Maybe it wasn't too late for them. Maybe he hadn't already completely screwed it all up.

"I need you, Keira. Can't imagine my life without you in it." He kissed her hard, quick. "We'll live here on the mountain if you want. Build our own place however you want it. I'll still have to travel, but I want you to go with me—only when you want to," he added. "It's up to you. I won't try to make plans without talking to you again. Won't tell you what to do—"

She laughed at his pained expression.

"Fine, I'll probably *still* tell you what to do. It's who I am. But you'll fight me on it because that's who you are. And it'll be good. Damn it, Keira, it'll be *great*. We'll be great. I need you so much. I want to show you the world. I want to give you everything you've ever wanted."

He paused for breath, gave her a half smile, swallowed what was left of his pride and admitted at last, "I'm just not sure how to do it without messing it all up. I've never loved anyone before, Keira. And I don't want to hurt you."

"I don't know what to say," she whispered, her voice breaking.

"Say you'll forgive me. Say you still love me," he urged before kissing her again, this time long and hard and deep. "Say you'll marry me, Keira."

"Nathan…" She laughed, reached up and grabbed hold of his hands, still on her face. "I can't believe you're here. Can't believe you're saying all of this. And I *do* love you. So much. Of course I'll marry you."

"Thank God," he said with a rush of breath. Grinning now, Nathan pulled her in close for a hug that nearly cracked her ribs. "It's your own fault, you know," he said, kissing her hair, resting his head atop hers. "You're the one who wouldn't let me stay on the outside. Now, you're just going to have to find a way to deal with having me on the *inside*."

She hugged him back, nestling in close, tucking her head beneath his chin. "I think I can handle that."

When he pulled back and held her at arm's length, he said, "I don't have a ring to give you, yet. We can go now—wait. Damn it, the lodge thing. I can't leave for a few more days."

She laughed. It sounded wonderful to him, the sweetest music Nathan could ever remember hearing.

"I don't need a ring right this minute," she said.

"I *need* you to have one," he told her, grinning as he suddenly saw the rest of his life stretch out in front of him, bright and beautiful. "The biggest damn diamond we can find. No, wait. Not one. Two diamonds. Or three or four. We'll look."

She laughed even harder and leaned into him to wrap her arms tightly around him, and Nathan sighed, completely content to stand here with her pressed against him forever. Just feeling her heart beat in tandem with his made him feel that his life was finally the way it should be.

Whispering now, he said, "I promise you, Keira, I will spend the rest of my life loving you and I will do everything I can to make you happy."

"I'm happier now than I've ever been, Nathan," she said, cuddling closer, holding him. "I will love you forever, and we'll make each other happy. I know we will. And I swear, you'll never be on the outside again. Neither of us will be."

He kissed her, feeling the magic, the rightness of it, and knew that for the first time in his life, Nathan Barrister had finally found home.

At the end of the month, Keira was practically dancing in place, impatient to board Nathan's private jet for their trip to Barbados—after a quick stop in London to visit Kelly. Before hoisting their bags, Nathan taped a note to the wall in the foyer of the lodge where his life had changed forever.

Luke,
It's been a hell of a month. Turns out, the middle of nowhere isn't exactly the black hole I thought it was. I hope you get as much out of your time here as I have.
Nathan

Then he left his past behind and hurried out to keep his future from breaking her leg in a fall.

* * * * *

The MILLIONAIRE OF THE MONTH series
continues with Christie Ridgway's
HIS FORBIDDEN FIANCÉE,
available April 2007
from Silhouette Desire.

Turn the page for a sneak preview of
IF I'D NEVER KNOWN YOUR LOVE
by
Georgia Bockoven

From the brand-new series
Harlequin Everlasting Love
Every great love has a story to tell. ™

One year, five months and four days missing

There's no way for you to know this, Evan, but I haven't written to you for a few months. Actually, it's been almost a year. I had a hard time picking up a pen once more after we paid the second ransom and then received a letter saying it wasn't enough. I was so sure you were coming home that I took the kids along to Bogotá so they could fly home with you and me, something I swore I'd never do. I've fallen in love with Colombia and the people who've opened their hearts to me. But fear is a constant companion when I'm there. I won't ever expose our children to that kind of danger again.

I'm at a loss over what to do anymore, Evan.

I've begged and pleaded and thrown temper tantrums with every official I can corner both here and at home. They've been incredibly tolerant and understanding, but in the end as ineffectual as the rest of us.

I try to imagine what your life is like now, what you do every day, what you're wearing, what you eat. I want to believe that the people who have you are misguided yet kind, that they treat you well. It's how I survive day to day. To think of you being mistreated hurts too much. If I picture you locked away somewhere and suffering, a weight descends on me that makes it almost impossible to get out of bed in the morning.

Your captors surely know you by now. They have to recognize what a good man you are. I imagine you working with their children, telling them that you have children, too, showing them the pictures you carry in your wallet. Can't the men who have you understand how much your children miss you? How can it not matter to them?

How can they keep you away from us all this time? Over and over, we've done what they asked. Are they oblivious to the depth of their cruelty? What kind of people are they that they don't care?

I used to keep a calendar beside our bed next to the peach rose you picked for me before you left. Every night I marked another day, counting how many you'd been gone. I don't do that any longer. I don't want to be reminded of all the days we'll never get back.

When I can't sleep at night, I tell you about my

day. I imagine you hearing me and smiling over the details that make up my life now. I never tell you how defeated I feel at moments or how hard I work to hide it from everyone for fear they will see it as a reason to stop believing you are coming home to us.

And I couldn't tell you about the lump I found in my breast and how difficult it was going through all the tests without you here to lean on. The lump was benign—the process reaching that diagnosis utterly terrifying. I couldn't stop thinking about what would happen to Shelly and Jason if something happened to me.

We need you to come home.

I'm worn down with missing you.

I'm going to read this tomorrow and will probably tear it up or burn it in the fireplace. I don't want you to get the idea I ever doubted what I was doing to free you or thought the work a burden. I would gladly spend the rest of my life at it, even if, in the end, we only had one day together.

You are my life, Evan.

I will love you forever.

* * * * *

Don't miss this deeply moving
Harlequin Everlasting Love story
about a woman's struggle to bring back
her kidnapped husband from Colombia and her
turmoil over whether to let go, finally, and
welcome another man into her life.
IF I'D NEVER KNOWN YOUR LOVE
by Georgia Bockoven
is available March 27, 2007.

And also look for
THE NIGHT WE MET
by Tara Taylor Quinn,
a story about finding love
when you least expect it.

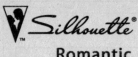

Romantic
SUSPENSE

*Excitement, danger
and passion guaranteed!*

USA TODAY bestselling author
Marie Ferrarella
is back with the second installment
in her popular miniseries,
*The Doctors Pulaski: Medicine
just got more interesting...*
DIAGNOSIS: DANGER is on sale
April 2007 from Silhouette®
Romantic Suspense (formerly
Silhouette Intimate Moments).

*Look for it wherever
you buy books!*

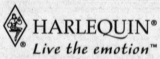

Introducing talented new author

TESSA RADLEY

*making her Silhouette Desire debut
this April with*

BLACK WIDOW BRIDE

Book #1794
Available in April 2007.

Wealthy Damon Asteriades had no choice but to
force Rebecca Grainger back to his family's estate—
despite his vow to keep away from her seductive
charms. But being so close to the woman society once
dubbed the Black Widow Bride had him aching to
claim her as his own...at any cost.

On sale April from Silhouette Desire!

Available wherever books are sold,
including most bookstores, supermarkets,
discount stores and drugstores.

COMING NEXT MONTH

#1789 MISTRESS OF FORTUNE—Kathie DeNosky
Dakota Fortunes
A casino magnate seeks revenge on his family by seducing his brother's stunning companion and daring her to become Fortune's mistress.

#1790 BLACKHAWK'S AFFAIR—Barbara McCauley
Secrets!
What's a woman to do when she comes face-to-face with the man who broke her heart years before…and realizes he's still her husband?

#1791 HER FORBIDDEN FIANCÉE—Christie Ridgway
Millionaire of the Month
He'd been mistaken for his identical twin before—but now his estranged sibling's lovely fiancée believes he's the man she wants to sleep with.

#1792 THE ROYAL WEDDING NIGHT—Day Leclaire
The Royals
Deceived at the altar, a prince sleeps with the wrong bride. But after sharing the royal wedding night with his mystery woman, nothing will stop him from discovering who she really is.

#1793 THE BILLIONAIRE'S BIDDING—Barbara Dunlop
A hotel heiress vows to save her family's business from financial ruin at any cost. Then she discovers the price is marrying her enemy.

#1794 BLACK WIDOW BRIDE—Tessa Radley
He despised her. He desired her. And the billionaire was just desperate enough to blackmail her back into his life.

SDCNM0307